wondrous
oblivion

wondrous
oblivion

Paul Morrison
Based on his original screenplay

Hodder
Children's
Books

A division of Hodder Headline Limited

Lyrics of 'Sugar Dandy' reproduced by permission
of Notting Hill Music

Lyrics of 'Dancin' Mood' reproduced by permission
of Sony Music Entertainment (UK) Limited

Extract quoted on page 137
from *Beyond a Boundary* by C. L. R. James

A Catalogue record for this book is available
from the British Library

ISBN 0 340 88405 3

Typeset in Palatino by Avon DataSet Ltd,
Bidford-on-Avon, Warwickshire

Printed and bound in Great Britain by
Bookmarque Ltd, Croydon, Surrey

The paper and board used in this paperback by
Hodder Children's Books are natural recyclable products
made from wood grown in sustainable forests.
The manufacturing processes conform to the environmental
regulations of the country of origin.

Hodder Children's Books
a division of Hodder Headline Ltd
338 Euston Road
London NW1 3BH

For Corey, Jacob and Joel

one

David stood idly in his baggy white shorts at the far boundary. The sun was shining, the clouds scudding across the sky. His shirt was whiter than white, and he prided himself on having the most brilliantly white boots on the field. The team trials had been going on for a while, but the ball had yet to come his way.

He tried out various postures that would demonstrate alertness: a cowboy about to draw his guns; a tiger-like crouch; erect like a guardsman. But the truth was that his mind was beginning to wander.

It wandered back to a newsreel he had seen in the cinema with his mother the previous weekend. The black and white images flickered in his mind's eye: Freddie Trueman flinging down a ball at furious speed; Colin Cowdrey, the batsman and England's cricket captain, stroking the ball away elegantly and taking a run.

David recalled the commentary, in the Queen's most plummy English: *'It's spring again, and that can* mean only one thing. Twenty-two men, good and true, a trusty willow and a leather ball. Howzat! Yes, the new cricket season is under way.'

The commentator's voice echoed in David's brain, the way it dropped to a reverential whisper. 'For the heroes of the game, like Trueman and Cowdrey, it's business as usual.' David began to improvise. 'But here at one of England's less fashionable venues, the selectors have their eye on a rising star. Yes it's David Wiseman, brilliant batsman, tactical genius, and as always, perfectly turned out. Can English cricket ignore this young talent a moment longer?'

David smiled contentedly.

Suddenly there was a loud clout of bat on ball. Howls went up from the distant figures around the bat. 'Wiseman!' 'Quickly!' 'Stop it!'

The newsreel juddered to a grinding halt. David pinched himself to see the ball rolling remorselessly towards him. He ran towards it, thought better of it, stopped, ran a little to the left. The ball continued its journey mercilessly. David hesitated, then sidestepped back to the right. The ball trundled on slowly and deliberately. David stooped down to grab it, but somehow the ball eluded him, passing between hand and foot. He turned abruptly and made a heroic last-minute dive. Full-length and positively graceful.

Nose to the turf, he watched the ball trickle gently over the boundary rope.

'Oh no!'

'Blithering idiot.'

'Typical.'

The groans of disappointment rang out from the bowler and other fielders, together with ironic laughter and applause from the opposing batsmen gathered at the edge of the field.

David retrieved the ball. He appeared oblivious to the uproar, and ran eagerly towards the wicket, holding the ball before him like the crown jewels. He shaped up to return it, happy to be involved.

Meanwhile the umpire, Mr Pugh, a teacher at David's prep school, had signalled four runs with his usual ex-army precision, and called 'Over!' The team began to swap ends. David was still looking for a bowler to throw the ball to, but everyone was on the move, and looking in the other direction. David spat on the ball, and rubbed it on his trousers. Boys who had reached their positions grinned as he passed them. His legendary enthusiasm was comically at odds with his equally renowned incompetence. David finally reached the centre of the pitch, and lobbed the ball eagerly to the next bowler. The boy scowled as the ball fell short, and trickled towards him.

Mr Pugh eyed David bemusedly.

'Are you enjoying your afternoon, Wiseman?'

'Yes, sir. Very much, sir.'

'Wondrous.'

David stood nodding eagerly, not knowing what was expected of him. Mr Pugh nodded back, mesmerised. Then he remembered where he was and what he was supposed to be doing. 'Back on the job then, boy!'

David turned and half-walked, half-trotted towards the boundary. Pugh called after him. 'All the way, boy!' David beamed a proud smile back towards him.

'Wondrous oblivion!' Pugh exclaimed, while the bowler sighed and polished up the ball impatiently, and the batsmen shook their heads in disbelief.

David took up his position on the outfield, a distant white dot at the edge of green.

* * *

David sat squashed in a compartment with the other travellers, mostly commuters returning from working in the city. The train rumbled over the great river Thames. He looked up from his Wisden scorebook while the familiar gasometers rolled by. Undeterred by the afternoon's events, he resumed the commentary so rudely interrupted.

'As potentially the greatest all-rounder the game has ever seen wends his way home to South London, cricket fans look forward to the coming season with eager anticipation. Let's hope 1960 will be a year to remember.'

David skipped past the corner tobacco shop, narrowly missing knocking over an emerging elderly lady, and scampered up the drab but respectable terraced street to home.

'The best of British luck, young David!'

two

David pulled his cricket shorts from his kit-bag and laid them out with a flourish on the ironing board. They sported a large green grass-stain. Ruth Wiseman feigned concern. 'What happened?'

'I dived,' said David with pride.

Ruth was a good-looking young woman, who tried her best to fit in. Her plain clothes attempted unsuccessfully to make her look older than her years. Her cultivated English betrayed the slight accent of a German refugee.

'Dived?'

'I dived for the ball. To stop it.'

Ruth fetched him a glass of milk from the fridge. She was always giving him glasses of milk. He rarely got to finish one before another landed before him. Milk meant more than a drink to Ruth. Milk meant health. Milk meant life.

'You dived for the ball?' she said. 'Clever. Do you play cricket in the swimming pool now?'

'No, Ma.'

'If you don't play in a field any more, should I get

you some swimming trunks to play cricket in?'

'No, Ma.'

Ruth liked to banter with her son. He was perhaps the only person in the world she felt safe enough to banter with. David picked up the shorts and looked at them worriedly.

'Will the stain come out?' he asked.

Ruth grabbed back the shorts and peered closely. 'It'll come out.'

'Wondrous.'

David grabbed the kit-bag and hurtled through the hallway and up the stairs. On the second step he called back to his mother, 'Wondrous oblivion!' By the ninth step, he could see into the open door of his precocious younger sister's room. Lillian was grinding out a mournful cello piece. On the twelfth step David clapped his hands to his ears. Lillian frowned fiercely. By the top, eighteen steps, she had kicked the door shut. Thank God for that. David dived into his room.

David's bedroom was at the rear of the terraced house, with one window looking out onto the gardens behind, and one overlooking next door's back extension. He'd arranged his most precious possessions around a small bookcase. Above it hung his two autographed pictures of cricket stars, on top of it was his cricket ball, by the side of it was his precious Surrey bat, complete with signatures of the team, and in it he displayed an array of cricket books. On the linoleum floor he was playing with the pride of his collection: his shoe box full of cricket cards, hundreds of them, given away free with packets of cigarettes, all pictures of English cricketers.

He took a bunch of cards in his hands and purposefully laid them out on the floor to create teams, eleven a side. He used his hushed commentator voice. *'The captains have made their selection and the teams are making their way onto the pitch.'*

Warm applause filled the air. David selected a card out of his hand. Dog-eared and dirty, it showed a Victorian cricketer with a huge beard, W.G. Grace, the father of the modern game. *'Grace, you have to umpire, you're too old to play.'* Grace scowled back at him. *'And no cheek either.'*

He pulled a card out from one of the teams on the floor, and slipped into the role of captain, brusque, authoritative, like Mr Pugh. *'Trueman, you can open the bowling. Fast bowlers first.'* Trueman gave him the thumbs up. Trueman would expect no less than to open the bowling.

He slid down a card from the other team, Dennis Compton.

'OK, Compton, you're opening the batting. Ready?' The face in the card nodded enthusiastically.

David reverted to his commentary voice. '*Trueman to bowl.*'

He rolled a six-sided pencil on the lino. The pencil had numbers scratched into the wood.

'*Good one! It's going for a four. Well hit, Dennis.*' Dennis stopped running and lifted his bat to acknowledge the compliment.

'*Wait a minute. The fielder is diving for it. Has he got his hands to it? No he can't reach it. Hard cheese. The umpire signals a four.*'

Grace motioned his arm to signal four runs, the crowd cheered, and David wrote furiously on his scorecard.

Outside a dog yapped excitedly. David rushed to the window. A tiny Yorkshire terrier scampered excitedly up and down the next-door garden.

'I'm here, Vinnie,' called David. 'I'm busy.'

Vinnie was David's best and only (living) friend in the neighbourhood. He got up on his hind legs and continued to yelp. David yelled back. 'OK, you win. Coming, Vinnie! I'll bring a treat for you.' He clattered down the stairs, grabbed something from the bathroom, and almost knocked his mum flat as they crossed in the kitchen. Ruth was on her way out to the front door with the milk bottles.

She leant down outside to put down the empties. A dark shadow fell across her. 'Mrs Wilson!' she gasped. The beefy, white-haired, and formidable Mrs Wilson was the matriarch of the street. She pushed her hard face close into Ruth's.

'Good evening, Mrs Wiseman,' she said.

'I didn't hear you. I wasn't expecting you.'

'I'm not stopping, Mrs Wiseman.'

Mrs Wilson's broad frame seemed to fill the tiny front garden. She looked round guardedly and lowered her voice. 'Do you have any idea who'll be moving in next door, Mrs Wiseman? When your friends go.'

Ruth turned pale. 'I've got no idea, Mrs Wilson.'

'I thought you might know who'll be moving in. I thought you might prefer one of your own people.'

'I never even thought about it, Mrs Wilson. I doubt if it's let yet.' She shivered. Mrs Wilson's questions sounded well-meaning enough, but there was something in her tone . . .

Ruth lowered her milk bottles. Mrs Wilson leant into her ear. 'Your petunias are coming on nicely,' she hissed. 'Such a pretty plant, don't you think?'

Ruth fumbled with a milk bottle, and it crashed to the ground.

Meanwhile at the back of the house David had scrambled over the fence and was on his knees on the lawn of the next-door garden. He was using a pink-handled hairbrush to stroke the quivering Vinnie. A plaintive pop ballad played on a distant record player. It was beginning to get dark.

A little toddler watched from the window, as David chatted away to the dog. 'You're a genius, Vinnie, that's what you are. What do you think of Trueman's form? Shall we keep him in the team?'

All these questions were beyond Vinnie. His excitement got the better of him. He leapt up, seized the brush from David, and, gripping it between his teeth, trotted away into a pile of scattered tea-chests. David stumbled after him. 'Hey! Come out, Vinnie. Give it back.'

The dog vanished into the boxes. David stood, helpless, in the falling light. 'Please, Vinnie. Where are you?' The boy in the window broke into laughter. David shrugged at him ruefully.

He scrambled over the fence and made his way through the back door. Victor, his father, stocky and forceful, had arrived home. Victor put down his cardboard box of accounts books. Ruth tried to help him to peel off his overcoat. It was a warm day, but he still liked to wear his overcoat to work. 'Don't fuss me,' he said to Ruth grumpily, in his Polish accent. Victor was in one of those moods. David slipped quietly up the stairs.

three

David was woken early next morning by the banging and scraping of furniture. He threw on his school uniform, gobbled down his Weetabix and rushed out of the door. A large removal van was parked outside. Workmen crashed out of the next-door house carrying furniture and tea-chests. Vinnie whined pitifully as his world was torn to pieces. David watched open-mouthed. So it was really happening. His mother had mentioned something in passing but it never hit him until now: the only other Jewish family in Duchess Road – and more importantly their dog – leaving.

The Glucksteins gathered in front of the newly erected 'TO LET' sign to watch their worldly goods disappear into the van. Ruth came running down the front steps past the bewildered David. She handed Mrs Gluckstein a tin.

'Dora, some biscuits to keep you going.'

'Oh, Ruth. You shouldn't have.'

'We're going to miss you so much.'

'We'll miss you, too.'

Ruth handed David his satchel. 'Now say goodbye to Anthony and Suzanne,' she told him. David stared blankly at the scene. Ruth turned to Victor who had followed her out.

'Did you talk to him?' she whispered.

Victor scowled at her. 'Did you?'

Ruth urged David, 'Come on now, give them a kiss.'

David pulled himself together and mechanically kissed the two small children on the forehead. 'Goodbye, Suzanne. Goodbye, Anthony.' He picked up Vinnie, who immediately stopped whining and rested his head meekly on David's shoulder.

'Aren't they sweet together,' said Mrs Gluckstein. 'You'll come and visit, David, won't you?'

David turned questioningly to his father, who had decided he had better act more genially in company, and that he ought to release the information his son required. 'They have their own house now, David. Mr Gluckstein has had a promotion.'

'And Vinnie?'

'Vinnie gets promoted too. To a better class of neighbourhood. Bigger trees.' Reluctantly David put Vinnie down.

Ruth plucked the dog-hairs off David's blazer.

'Button up your coat, darling. Don't make yourself late, now.'

He sighed. She made him wear his coat if there was just a slight breath of wind in the air – even on the sunniest day. David turned and started up the road.

The two families called after him, 'Goodbye, David. Goodbye.'

Halfway up the street he turned and shouted, 'Goodbye, Vinny.'

The dog barked a frantic response.

Equally frantically, David waved back.

* * *

David's prep school was on the north side of the river and very upmarket. He had had to take a difficult test to get in two years previously, and it cost his father a pretty penny to keep him there. The idea had been that he would have a better start in life than his parents. But it wasn't David's idea, and, partly because none of the other boys lived in his area, he hadn't yet made any friends.

The assembled school, bored and tuneless, were laying into the morning hymn.

'Praise my soul the king of heaven.
Praise the everlasting king.

Ransomed, healed, restored, forgiven.

To his feet thy tribute bring.'

The hymn filtered through to those boys who were excused from Christian worship. They waited in empty silence in a nearby classroom. Most of them were Jewish, one was a sandal-wearing committed atheist. David sat next to the only Indian boy, Vikram Singh, and thumbed through a handful of cigarette cards abstractedly.

'Praise him, praise him.

Praise him, praise him.

Praise with us the God of grace.'

The hymn screeched to a halt. David and the other non-Christians filed in awkwardly to the back of the hall for the daily announcements, exposed in their difference and separateness. One boy, Jessop, gave the Nazi salute as David passed.

'Sieg Heil,' he whispered.

'Shut up, Jessop,' said Reece, the round-faced boy next to him.

At the front of the hall stood the head teacher, gaunt and balding, accompanied by the four housemasters. He was talking about David's favourite subject.

'I have great pleasure in announcing that this year's new captain of cricket will be James Reece, who did so splendidly for us last year, both at the crease, and as a bowler.'

The school applauded, none more enthusiastically than David, as Reece walked coolly to the front to take his place at the right hand of the head. 'I expect the whole school to give Reece every possible support, and to turn out to cheer the team in home games. Last year, you'll recall, we were second in the Junior Challenge Cup. This year we intend to bag it.'

Reece returned proudly to his seat, amid much backslapping from the prospective members of the team. David watched the bonhomie wistfully from a distance. The head continued. 'For the rest of you triallists, Mr Pugh will post the team sheets on the notice-board tomorrow.'

So all was not yet lost. Maybe not captain. But there was still a chance he was in *one* of the teams, if not the actual first eleven. David could see his name on the team-sheet already.

'Dismiss!' bellowed the head.

Reece and the other hot prospects left the ancient hall, arms draped around one another's shoulders. They headed off down the corridor in a gaggle. David followed at a distance, full of new hope.

* * *

The Wiseman emporium was a well stocked and flourishing drapery and linen store. As the proprietor argued about a missing order on the telephone in the back office, Ruth was up a ladder stacking rolls of cloth. David stood at the end of the counter, facing George Woodberry, a chain-smoking sales rep.

Woodberry was a regular visitor to Victor's shop. He held a small pile of cigarette cards in the palm of his hand and was laying them out one by one on the counter. David's eyes were glued to the cards.

'Here,' said Mr Woodberry. 'Bailey, Essex.'

'Got him.'

'Trueman, Yorkshire.'

'Of course.'

Mr Woodberry eyed David quizzically. 'You're as hard to please as your father. Here's one you won't have. Benaud. New South Wales.'

David smiled victoriously, from ear to ear.

'You haven't! You young scamp!'

David swelled with pride. Woodberry blew a perfect smoke-ring and leant in close.

'All right. How about this one?' He slapped the card hard on the counter. 'Jones. Glamorgan. The wicket-keeper.'

The smile disappeared from David's face, and his

desire became palpable. Woodberry scented blood. He enjoyed tormenting his client's son.

'You want it, don't you?'

'Yes. Please, Mr W.'

'I've actually got something you want. A miracle.' He lowered his voice conspiratorially. 'Well, what have you got for me, young David? What are you going to do for me?'

David looked around helplessly.

'Swaps?'

'Swaps, David. Very Jewish, that is. What would I do with swaps?' He shook his head pitilessly. David's eyes begged.

Mr Woodberry burst into laughter. 'They are yours, son. Of course they are yours. What would I do with them? On the house! We're friends, aren't we?'

He tipped a wink towards Victor. This was surely worth another commission. David shuffled through the new cards, transfixed.

'Thanks, Mr Woodberry.'

four

David had been hoping to get upstairs and back to his new cards straight after dinner. But when the dishes were cleared, Victor had insisted on adapting the dining table as a workbench. He organised the family into a production line, making up cushion covers from short ends of material. Lillian pinned on the paper template, Victor cut, Ruth sewed on her Singer, and David stuffed cushions into the covers. Victor kept them going like the clappers.

Ruth's mind was still on Mrs Wilson. She hissed at Victor over the whir of the machine.

'Surely we would prefer our own people, she said.'

'So? Good!'

'Not good. I don't like it. It's not her business, who's going to live next door.'

'Nothing to worry. This is England. You think this is Germany? This is England. They have a democracy here. Freedom.'

David's attention wandered to Victor's newspaper, lying upside-down on a chair. David screwed up his head to read the back page headline.

His reverie was interrupted by his mother flinging another cushion at him. He tried sharing his own news.

'Reece was made captain of cricket.'

'Nice for Mr Reece,' said Victor. 'How come they didn't choose you?'

'I was in the trials. I could still be vice-captain.'

Lillian raised her eyebrows dubiously. She might be the younger one, but she had limited respect for her brother's abilities. Lillian and Victor took the position of the realists in this family, Ruth and David the dreamers. But the difference between Ruth and David was that Ruth was also a worrier. Her sewing machine clattered away. She tore the cotton thread with her teeth.

'Didn't they have a democracy in Germany too?' she said. 'Who was it voted for Hitler?'

'Mrs Wilson?' countered Victor.

'All the Mrs Wilsons. Ordinary citizens. Wasn't it? Gentiles. Who voted for Hitler.'

For once, beaten in argument, Victor chose insult. 'No comparison. Don't be stupid.'

Ruth turned away, flattened. Victor switched off the machine.

'Enough! Time for bed.'

David sat in his pyjamas at the bedroom window, methodically applying whitener to his cricket boots with an old toothbrush. They gleamed in the dim light. Tomorrow was notice-board day, and then games in the afternoon. He was going to be ready, for anything.

Ruth entered softly. She held out the white woollen sleeve she had been knitting.

'Put out your arm,' she said.

David complied and she held the sleeve against him. She showed him the knitting pattern with a picture of Dennis Compton in a white sweater on the front. 'See? The same exactly,' she said. 'You'll be the smartest boy in the team.'

'Thanks, Mum.'

Ruth stood a moment, quiet, a little awkward. She glanced down at the floor, awash with cricket teams.

'Shall I tidy your cards?'

'No. Leave them. Thanks, Mum.'

David returned to his cricket boots. Ruth slipped out of the door. Someone with a squeaky mower was cutting the grass further down the street. An Elvis Presley ballad wafted across the back gardens, the deep echoing voice filled with yearning.

From outside the house David looked like a midget, sitting with his boots on his lap, head and feet so close. He stood to his full height and gazed out at the factory opposite, quiet and mysterious, and the empty garden next door.

Lillian's voice drifted up the stairs to David's room.

'Where's Dad?'

He could faintly hear his mother's answer. 'He took the cushions. To the shop.'

'Have you seen my hairbrush? It's vanished. I can't find it anywhere . . .'

David sighed.

* * *

'Yes! Run!' called Reece.

The batsmen thundered down the pitch. It was a perfect day for cricket. David was glowing in full kit. But he wasn't in a team, or even on the field. The trip to the notice-board hadn't produced the result he had imagined. He was sitting next to the scoreboard, a contraption mounted on an easel with numbers that flipped over marking the score.

The batsmen clustered nearby clapped and cheered enthusiastically.

Mr Heath, umpiring, signalled two runs and watched keenly as David flipped over the numbers. David looked proud, anxious, and utterly immersed in his task. He pointed his gaze stiffly back towards the umpire.

Mr Pugh's shadow fell over him.

'Well done, Wiseman. You've a head for numbers at least. We'll make this a regular job, shall we?'

'Yes, sir.'

Pugh began to move on, then had a second thought.

'No need to wear whites . . .'

He saw David's crestfallen face.

'. . . if you don't want to.'

five

David sauntered home, kit-bag in hand. It could have been worse. At least he got to go to matches and wear his kit. He pondered the relative merits of Tyson, Statham and Trueman as fast bowlers. Who to pick tonight as his two openers?

He rounded the corner shop to see a battered old truck parked in front of the house next door to theirs. The 'TO LET' sign had been ripped off the gatepost and lay slewed over the hedge. Voices emerged from the open front door.

He dashed excitedly up the street, almost falling over a brightly coloured sofa waiting on the pavement. He let himself in and scampered up the hallway to the kitchen. 'Mum! We've got neighbours again!'

Ruth and Lillian were huddled over the kitchen table. Inside the shouting and laughing from next door were louder, the thumps and bangs of furniture being heaved around.

Ruth's face was pale and drawn. Lillian's was angry.

'How am I going to get any practice done with all this going on?' she groaned.

There was a rattling and crashing noise as the back door opposite was unlocked and burst open. David rushed to the kitchen window and jumped up eagerly to see above the fence. He caught a quick glimpse of a black face, a bucket of water being sloshed into the drain. A broad West Indian woman's voice shouted back into the house.

'Loretta! Come see now!'

David desperately tried, ballerina-like, to balance on the end of his toes. He glimpsed the woman with the bucket, round and friendly looking, being joined by another, younger woman.

'Look at the size of this yard!' the younger woman exclaimed. 'Good, eh?'

Ruth pulled David back down.

'Don't be rude,' she said. 'You mustn't stare at people.'

'I just wanted to see who it was.'

'Well you've seen now. That's enough.'

'Not properly. Are they Africans? They talk English. They aren't Indians. I know that. They aren't red Indians.'

Ruth placed herself between David and the

window and made herself frantically busy at the sink. David charged off upstairs. Ruth's eyes wandered unbidden to the window.

The two women were heading for the garden. 'I'm going to pick some flowers for the girls' room,' said the older one. 'Fetch me a knife.'

David peeked cautiously round his bedroom curtain. The older woman was cutting flowers with a kitchen knife. The younger one, perhaps a grown-up daughter, took the flowers and made them into a bunch. Their clothes and smiles were bright, not like most of the women he knew.

David shrank back. Two other black women, one tall and grey-haired, the other small and carrying a broom and duster, were emerging from the house. A man followed them, skinny and wearing a pork-pie hat.

'Mr Johnson!' said the mother. 'I didn't know you here too.'

He looked around him. 'Very nice, Mrs Samuels,' he said. 'Good for you.'

'Yes indeed.' The two women echoed his sentiments.

'Where's the toilet, Mrs Samuels?' he asked with a grin.

'Inside, Mr Johnson. Inside.'

'You won't catch cold in the winter, then!' he said. They all laughed. David's ears were flapping.

The tall woman asked, 'What time the children coming?'

Mrs Samuels checked her watch. 'My gosh,' she said. 'Mustn't be late. Loretta, put these flowers in water. Dennis coming from work in a hour or so.'

She scuttled off. 'Back soon!'

The others made their way back inside. David reluctantly unglued his nose from the window. This was more than interesting. This was earth-shattering.

The sounds from next door subsided, and David got on with the game he'd been planning. The cricketers in the cards did their best to entertain. But David could scarcely concentrate. Before long his attention was drawn once more to voices raised in the garden. A woman and a man. An argument. He peeped out once more. The daughter was marching back into the house. A tall, broad-shouldered man in a working-man's boiler suit called after her.

'Don't be like that, Loretta. We still got room for Mama's roses.'

'You better, Dad!' she called over her shoulder.

The big man – maybe the father – shrugged at Mr Johnson, still in his pork-pie hat. Mr Johnson shrugged back. The big man had a strong, lived-in face. Like a picture of a boxer David had once seen. Joe Louis. He glanced up at David. David walked airily across the room. He didn't want the men to think he was spying on them.

He allowed himself another peek. The two men were on their knees, crawling up each side of the garden, feeling the turf, pointing and gesticulating. Then together they paced the length of the lawn. At the far end the big man gave a cheer of delight, and slapped Mr Johnson on the back gleefully. Mr Johnson pretended to be knocked for six, then with a flourish handed the big man a garden fork.

The big man worked away at the island of rose bushes that occupied the middle of the lawn, the central feature of the garden. David watched with fascination as he strained to uproot the tough old bushes. As he threw each bush aside, with its large head of gnarled root, Mr Johnson gingerly picked it up, and carried it off towards the house.

Suddenly a car hooted loudly. Loretta called from the kitchen. 'Dennis!'

Mr Johnson dropped his rosebush. 'The girls,' he exclaimed. 'They're here.'

The big man hesitated a moment, threw down the fork, drew a deep breath, and strode swiftly back to the house.

David sprinted from his room and across the landing to his parents' bedroom. Lillian was already there. They gazed through the net curtain.

A taxi was drawn up out front. The driver was wrestling with the battered suitcases. Mrs Samuels, the mother, emerged from the back, followed by a chubby black man with a dog collar, and two girls, one about David's age and one younger, wide-eyed and wondering, in matching yellow dresses and matching pigtails.

The big man advanced to greet them.

'Look at you. Judy. Dorothy. So grown up.'

They looked back up at him shyly.

He leant down to the little one and asked, 'You remember me, Dorothy?'

She shook her head. The big man's face fell.

'You remember me, Judy?'

'Yes,' said the older girl.

The big man's eyes began to water. David looked away to the street. 'Look at all the neighbours,' he said to Lillian, open-mouthed. He had never seen such a buzz. Mrs Wilson was clipping her already perfect hedge. Mrs Dunkley had frozen rigid on the way back from the corner shop. Mrs Roberts was putting out the milk bottles, and another couple were emptying their rubbish. Net curtains were twitching all along the street. Anyone would think the Queen had arrived.

'I bet I can't lift you up,' said the big man to the girls. 'I bet I can't lift you up.' He grabbed one of them in each arm, swung them round and hugged them to him.

'We got our children back, Dennis,' said Mrs Samuels. Mrs Wilson's shears snapped furiously.

six

Victor flushed the chain and emerged from the bathroom. 'Give me a piece of bread while I'm waiting,' he demanded. 'I could eat a horse tonight.'

'It's on the table,' said Ruth.

The Wiseman bathroom was at the far end of the kitchen on the ground floor, a hangover from the days when the toilet had been outside the house. David raced past his father and jumped up on the toilet seat to peer at the goings on out back through the bathroom window. His curiosity was undimmed.

Ruth's nerves were shot. Her hands were shaking as she poured the stew out of the saucepan and into a serving dish. The thump of music and raucous laughter carried through from next door.

'It's been like this all day,' Ruth said, as she, Victor and Lillian carried the dishes through to the dining room. 'I never thought for a minute . . .'

'They are unpacking, for God's sake!' replied Victor.

'Unpacking. And shouting. And singing. And laughing.'

37

'It's like a musical, Dad,' said Lillian. 'How do they get anything done?'

'It's all right for you,' said Ruth. 'You're not here. You can afford to be generous.'

'I'm here now,' said Victor. 'Do we get any dinner still?'

'DAVID!' yelled Ruth. David tore himself away from his perch on the toilet seat.

Ruth set the dish on the table. She looked up at the wall that joined the two houses. The sound seemed to swell and intensify. Shouting and crashing, music and singing, glasses clinking, the thump of the front door. Ruth's ornaments trembled. She turned to Victor.

'Aren't you going to do something?'

'Give them time. They've just arrived.'

Victor didn't want to be bothered. Victor was busy enough. He had his own plans. He didn't like to be interfered with. He had seen things as a soldier in the war that no-one should have to see. He didn't talk about them. This was nothing to compare with that, a storm in a teacup. Take no notice, was his policy. Avoid trouble.

Ruth bit her tongue, with difficulty, and started ladling out the stew.

David delivered the latest news from the garden. 'All the roses are out.'

Victor raised an eyebrow. 'Mrs Wilson will like that!'

'There are only three bedrooms,' piped up Lillian. 'How many of them do you think are going to live there?'

'Who knows?' replied Victor. 'Fifty?'

Ruth banged down her ladle.

'Do we only have one thing in the world to talk about?' she said. 'That's enough now. Find another topic please. You are all clever people. So talk clever, for God's sake. Talk about something else.'

The family stared at one another, nonplussed. Victor munched his bread without expression, then smiled ironically.

'You know what we can be thankful for?'

Ruth shook her head dubiously.

'Mrs Wilson. Your good Mrs Wilson. All the Mrs Wilsons. They won't have time to think about us yids any more.'

The wall quivered.

seven

David opened the front door and emerged into the daylight. The birds were chirping brightly; the milkman's bottles clinked further down the street. Suddenly he spotted something on the front path of the house next door. A large pile of manure. Smelly manure. Horse manure. Wasps buzzed around it excitedly.

'Phooaar!' he said.

Ruth followed him down the path, looking somewhat the worse for wear. David held his nose and pointed to the dung. Ruth slapped his hand down to his side.

'Oh my goodness!' she said. Mrs Dunkley, two doors up, leant over her gate pretending not to look.

The door to the next-door house opened, and out came the mother, wearing an old housecoat over her nurse's uniform. She was followed by the two girls, smartly dressed in white blouses and grey skirts. She carried two enormous bags of bottles, the debris of the night's celebrations. She apparently ignored the manure completely and ushered the wondering girls around it. Mrs Dunkley hid a nasty smile.

'Morning!' the West Indian mother called out to Ruth.

Ruth jumped out of her skin. 'Um . . . er . . . Good morning. Good morning.'

'Mrs . . . ?'

'Wiseman. Mrs Wiseman.'

'Mrs Wiseman, good morning.'

Ruth was struggling between her desire to flee, and her natural hospitality. The latter got the better of her.

'Good morning to you,' she replied.

The woman approached her. 'Sorry 'bout the noise last night. Our children came up from back home – Jamaica – and a few friends turn up to greet them. We never meant to have a party or, well, we would have invited you . . .'

Ruth interjected hastily. 'No. Yes. It's all right. Not to worry, Mrs . . .'

'Samuels. Mrs Samuels.' She ushered the girls forward. 'These are my girls. Judy, and Dorothy. Shake hands with the lady.' Ruth reached out a reluctant hand. Mrs Samuels added, 'I got a grown-up one, also.'

David retreated behind his mother. Mrs Samuels coughed politely. Ruth took the hint. 'Oh, yes. This is my boy, David.'

She pushed him out to shake hands.

Mrs Samuels asked, 'Where do you go to school, David?'

David went a deep shade of red. Suddenly he was completely unable to remember the name of his school. 'I . . . er . . .'

'He doesn't want to say,' interjected Mrs Samuels. 'Doesn't want to shame us, in his smart uniform.'

Judy smiled at him sympathetically. David sidled back behind his mother, out of Mrs Samuels' formidable eye-line.

Mrs Samuels put her arms around the girls. 'We just trying out the local school. Mustn't be late. A good education is the most important thing, don't you agree, Mrs Wiseman?'

She nodded at the pile of dung. 'Good for the garden, that.' She bustled the girls down the street past Mrs Dunkley.

Ruth stood frozen in wonder.

In an instant, she was surrounded. Mrs Wilson huffing and puffing on one side, the stick-thin Mrs Dunkley pecking away on the other.

'I hope you gave her a good talking to, Mrs Wiseman,' Mrs Dunkley said. 'We were up all night with that racket. What it must have been like for you, heaven alone knows.'

'Terrible. It was terrible.'

They watched Mrs Samuels and the two girls disappear round the corner.

'Why don't you complain to the landlord?' said Mrs Wilson. 'He's one of your people, isn't he?'

'Mr Simpson?' said Ruth. 'I don't know, Mrs Wilson. He's a nice fellow. But Jewish? I . . .'

'I am sure I heard it,' said Mrs Dunkley. 'That he was a Jew.'

'You'd think he'd have more concern for you,' said Mrs Wilson. 'He must have known what he was doing.'

'He's a businessman,' said Ruth. 'I never heard anyone say he's a Jewish person.'

'You find out, dear, and make a complaint,' said Mrs Dunkley. 'The noise. The smells.'

She turned her nose up at the manure. Mrs Wilson shook her head sadly. Ruth looked appealingly at the waiting David. He shrugged and backed off down the road.

Mrs Wilson drew herself up to her full height.

'I was born on this street,' she said. 'So were my children. We don't have a lot. But we'll defend what we've got. We didn't fight a war for nothing.'

'Indeed, Mrs Wilson,' said Ruth. 'Just what I was saying to my husband last night.'

Mrs Wilson and Mrs Dunkley exchanged bemused glances. Mrs Dunkley placed a friendly hand on Ruth's arm. 'We're relying on you, dear,' she said. 'To be a good Englishwoman.'

Ruth stood there, paralysed.

eight

Most evenings the big man was out working on the garden. But was he gardening? If so, it was a kind of gardening that the residents of Duchess Road were unable to recognise. Having removed the flower-beds, he had rearranged the turf, so that a central strip was fully grassed. As promised, the roses had been replanted along the far fence. Then he had spent a lot of time working on the grassy strip, mowing and rolling and watering with great care.

Ruth had done her best to avoid further contact, caught as she was between her natural goodwill and her fear of all the 'proper' Englishwomen who had somehow landed her with the job of driving out the newcomers. She had dealt with her dilemma so far by keeping her distance and doing nothing.

One evening the big man was working in the half-light, mowing and rolling the new lawn. Judy was raking, and picking up the cuttings. Mr Johnson leant easily against the back wall. 'Look like a heavy roller!' observed Mr Johnson.

'You want a go?' asked the big man.

'No, no, man,' Mr Johnson demurred.

Ruth was perched on a chair in the kitchen in the half-dark changing a light bulb. She had a good view over the fence. The big man wore a white singlet, muscles straining. In spite of herself, Ruth watched transfixed.

David entered quietly. 'Mum?'

Ruth covered up her curiosity. 'Pass me that bulb off the table, would you?' She handed David the old bulb and inserted the new one into the fitting. Instantly the light went on. Ruth was caught in its glare.

The light spilt into the next-door garden, stopping the big man in his tracks. His eyes caught Ruth's for a brief moment.

Ruth flushed. 'Help me down from here,' she asked David abruptly. She bustled across the kitchen to put the old bulb in the waste bin. Her back turned, David jumped up on the chair and peered over. Judy had grabbed hold of the handle of the roller, and was pulling with all her might. It didn't budge. Mr Johnson passed the big man a hip-flask. He took a healthy swig.

Mrs Samuels banged out of the back door and marched up the garden. Dennis hid the hip-flask behind his back. 'When you going to do some work inside this house, eh?' demanded Mrs Samuels. 'I one slavin' to get order in here.'

She reached out for the hip-flask. 'Here, give me that.'

'No, no, Grace. You can't have that.'

Mr Johnson hastily retrieved his flask. The big man called out, 'Pull, Judy. Pull.'

Judy lost her grip on the reluctant roller, and fell over backwards amid peals of laughter, legs waving in the air. David blushed and looked away.

Ruth, who had also been absorbed in the scene, finally noticed David up on the chair. 'Get down from there!' she said. 'Mind your own business. Can't you find anything better to do?'

'Yes, Mum,' he answered, stepping down.

'Well do it then!'

'Yes, Mum.'

She pondered for a moment. 'What *are* they doing there?' she whispered.

'I don't know, Mum.'

nine

David strolled down the school corridor, mulling over the previous day's match. It had been a bad afternoon for the first eleven. The middle order batting had collapsed, and the team had come close to losing a match they should have won easily. Only good bowling had rescued them. Pugh had bawled them out mercilessly. Some of them were in a real strop, fearing for their places. David had been a reluctant witness to all this. Now there was a funny mood around. Even David couldn't help noticing.

Rounding the corner, David heard a commotion coming from one of the classrooms. He got up on tiptoes and pressed his nose to the glass.

Inside, Jessop, the first team wicket-keeper, and some other boys were piling chairs and desks on top of one small boy pinned underneath.

Jessop beckoned to David. 'Come on, Wiseman. Bloom's in for it this time.'

David slipped inside. 'What did he do?'

'He's been a pain. Quick. Got to finish the job before a teacher comes.'

David hesitated. Bloom was Jewish like him. But not sporty at all, not even interested. He was pretending to laugh but he didn't sound very happy.

Jessop was losing patience with David. 'Are you with us or not?' he demanded.

'I've . . . got something else I have to do.'

A big, bulky boy, Fox paused in the act of lowering a table onto the growing pile. 'If you tell you get the same treatment, right?'

David nodded.

He slipped out and closed the door as Bloom's laughter turned to sobs. He glimpsed a teacher and beckoned to him ineffectually. 'Sir. Sir.'

The teacher strode on past.

* * *

That day was one of Ruth's shop days. David met her there from the train after school, and when she was ready they walked home together. Lillian went to a friend nearby. David didn't want to worry his mother about the day's events, so he chatted about mathematics. They rounded the corner shop into their street. Mrs Wilson came bundling up the road towards them, puffing and blowing.

'Mrs Wiseman, Mrs Wiseman!'

Ruth quickened her pace to that of a competition

sprint walker, dragging David along beside her. Mrs Wilson accelerated accordingly.

'What's the matter?' asked David.

Ruth kept her head down. 'Shut up.'

She swirled into the front gate with David in tow, and reached the front door just as Mrs Wilson arrived breathless at the gate.

'Any progress, Mrs Wiseman?'

Ruth fumbled with the key.

'Not yet, Mrs Wilson. But the noise is much reduced.'

Mrs Wilson didn't look convinced. 'Is it, Mrs Wiseman?'

She pushed David through the door. 'Much reduced. I do assure you.'

Ruth closed the door breathlessly behind her. David barged past her and bounded up the stairs.

The noise in the kitchen was deafening. A metallic clanging that reverberated in Ruth's ears. She slumped into a chair.

Upstairs, David pulled aside the curtain. In the next-door garden the big man had been busy again. With a large sledgehammer, he rhythmically and precisely pounded metal stakes into the lawn. The clash of steel on steel sliced through the neighbourhood.

The sweat ran down him. He stopped for a breather. Mr Johnson, always the life-support machine, handed him a beer.

Ruth lifted her eyes heavenwards. It was all beyond her.

ten

Music emanated from the kitchen of the house next door. A happy rollicking ska number that made David smile.

He had never seen the back gardens so busy, even on a weekend. The neighbours were gathered in clusters with the appearance of doing one thing – digging or pruning, hanging out washing, rocking the child in the pram – but with the real intent of finding out what was happening in the garden next to David's.

The big man was balanced heroically at the top of a rickety stepladder, holding the end of a piece of old and tattered netting. Wooden posts had been bolted to the ends of the stakes in the ground. Judy handed him a hammer and the big man thumped a nail into the top of a post. Then he hooked the netting on to the nail. Netting was already strung around three sides of the lawn, leaving only the 'house' side open.

The whole family were helping. Mrs Samuels was mending holes in the netting with a large needle.

She had the practised hands of a fisher-woman. Loretta was cutting up pieces of string and tying the netting to the posts. Mr Johnson held the bottom pegs, while Dorothy drove them into the ground with a mallet. It was a nice picture of collective endeavour.

The big man was coming to the climax of his efforts. Together he and Mr Johnson unfurled the last roll of netting to complete a roof. He banged in the final nail, and turned proudly to his wife.

'See, Grace.'

Mrs Samuels stepped back to admire their handiwork.

'Yes. Nice. Yes.'

David, watching wide-eyed, was startled by a voice beside him.

'Some raspberries this man thinks he's going to grow. Doesn't he know this is England?'

It was his father. 'Do you know what it is?'

David shook his head.

'Beans?' he tried.

'Not likely,' replied Victor. 'I could make a guess. But I won't. Let's watch a moment.'

The Samuels family put down their tools. Judy emerged from the back of the house carrying a cricket bat, a set of stumps, bails, and a ball. The family clapped and cheered. David practically jumped out of his skin.

'Dad! Look!'

'Meshuga.'

'It's a cricket net.'

Mr Johnson helped Judy hammer the stumps into the ground. She set the bails on top, while the big man loosened up his bowling arm.

Loretta took the bat first. The big man tossed a slow ball down to her. She prodded it gently back down the pitch.

'He's a spinner,' said David to his father.

'Our neighbours are a little naive,' replied Victor. 'They misunderstand the British values.'

Loretta handed the bat to Judy.

Victor continued. 'The Englishman's love of cricket only goes so far.' He nodded in the direction of an affronted Mrs Dunkley. 'Which is not so far as the Englishwoman's garden.'

Judy squared up at the crease. The big man stepped back for a longer run-up.

'It's going to be a fast one,' said David excitedly.

'Let's hope we are not caught in the middle,' mused Victor.

The big man sent down a ball with real pace in

it. Judy opened her shoulders, lifted her bat high, shifted her weight onto her back foot, and let go with a sweeping leg drive that sent the ball hurtling into the net towards David and his father.

'Duck!' shouted Victor, grabbing his son and dropping to the floor in one rapid motion. Not for nothing was Victor's training in the arts of war.

The ball plunged into the net, which distended almost to a point, then returned to normal as it held firm against the impact. The ball dropped to the ground.

It was a glorious shot. The Samuels family cheered mightily. The big man shouted, 'It worked, man. Did you see? It worked.'

David and his father picked themselves off the floor. David started to applaud. The Samuels glanced up at him. He dragged his father away from the window.

'They can see us.'

'OK, OK.' Victor said. 'Half the street is watching this spectacle.'

The big man was exultant. He hugged Judy. 'You sure gave it a good test, sweetheart.' He turned to his wife proudly. 'See, she hasn't lost her touch, has she?'

'Now you going to fix my kitchen,' she replied. 'You hear, Mr clever-dick Samuels.'

* * *

David hurtled into the kitchen, Victor following after.

'Mum! Mum!'

Ruth was sitting at the table with Lillian, shelling peas.

'Don't tell me, please. Don't tell me.'

'All that effort,' said Victor. 'And what for?'

'It's a cricket net,' said David.

'Really!' said Lillian scornfully.

Ruth looked with concern towards her husband.

eleven

At dinner-time, David was squirming with excitement. He couldn't keep away from that window, with the view of the net wafting temptingly in the breeze. Ruth carried a dish to the table.

'Come on, David,' she said. 'It's fish. Your favourite.'

David reluctantly tore himself away.

'It's a cheek,' said Lillian. 'Calling themselves Samuels. Samuels is a Jewish name.'

David was eager to find common ground. 'Are they Jewish?'

Lillian did her best to ignore him. 'It's after the prophet Samuel, isn't it?'

'The Jews gave the bible to all people,' replied Ruth. 'Isn't that true?'

'We gave too much,' said Victor. 'That's also true. I don't see so much gratitude around.'

Lillian looked witheringly at her brother. 'Say other people get the wrong idea. Like David. And think they are one of us.'

'Sobers,' mused David. 'Is Sobers a Jewish name too?'

'We aren't really Wiseman,' said Lillian. 'We're . . . Weissenkopf or something. You told me. We haven't got our own name. Thank goodness, I have to say.'

The children's chatter died. David's eyes drifted to the window. Victor looked meaningfully towards Ruth. She took a deep breath.

'You are not to start getting ideas . . . David, I'm speaking to you!'

David returned his gaze to his mother.

'You can talk,' she said, 'be polite, speak when someone speaks to you, but that's as far as it goes. Understand?'

David looked appealingly to his father. They had a cricket net in the next-door garden!

'These are not our kind of people,' Victor said. 'We have nothing against them. But we don't mix. Their habits are different. Their manners are different. Do I make myself clear?'

David nodded assent. His father couldn't be clearer.

Victor looked to his wife approvingly.

'Good,' he said.

Ruth felt a twinge of satisfaction. She did her best to be a good wife. It wasn't often that Victor seemed to appreciate her efforts.

'Now. Eat,' she said.

It was a full moon that night. The cricket cards were restless in their box. Something seemed to be calling to them.

The net shimmered silver in the moonlight.

The fine-cut turf glowed white. It hummed, as if with electricity.

The newly unveiled pitch stirred into being, energised by the collective memory of millions of eager cricketers, millions of games, billions of balls bowled, trillions of runs. The stumps quivered, and glistened with dew.

David tossed and turned in his sleep.

twelve

The rabbi's voice rang out with the beginning of the Amidah, the standing prayer. The small congregation rose from their tatty seats. There weren't enough Jews in this area of South London to build a synagogue, so they rented a dusty Methodist church hall. Most were men and boys, in prayer shawls and skullcaps, but a few women hid behind a gauze curtain and brought out the bread, wine and orange squash at the end of the service.

An older boy, Yasha, orthodox with long sideburns, leant over to David.

'Come to our discussion group after. They talk about sex. It's interesting.'

He handed David a leaflet. 'The Torah of Human Relations'.

David shook his head.

'Why waste your time on cricket, Wiseman?' said Yasha. 'You're a good scholar.'

David was coming up for his twelfth birthday. After that he would have to start preparing for his barmitzvah, when he would have to read to the congregation from the holy scrolls. His father had reluctantly started giving up a morning in the shop once a month to get him used to being in *shul*. Victor wasn't a religious man – he couldn't understand where God had been when some of the things he had witnessed in the war had occurred. But he believed in keeping tradition, and it was a matter of some frustration to him that the Jewish Sabbath was on his busiest day.

On the other side of Victor from David stood Mr Silverstein, a skinny fellow with a large and humorous nose. Silverstein tired of mumbling the prayer at breakneck speed. He whispered in Victor's ear.

'How are your new neighbours?'

Victor's serenity was disturbed. 'Who told you?'

'A little bird. A blackbird, in fact.'

'It's not a problem.' Victor thumbed rapidly through his prayer book. 'Where are we?'

Silverstein gave him another nudge.

'Until you want to sell, maybe. Then it's a problem.'

'Sell?' Victor exclaimed. 'I should be so lucky to have a house to sell.'

Suddenly pious, he returned with a loud and

strong voice into the prayer. Silverstein raised his eyebrows incredulously at David. But David's mind was somewhere else . . .

* * *

'I went to a lot of trouble. These won't come cheap, you know!'

Back in the shop after the service, David was in serious negotiation with Mr Woodberry. He'd put in his request days ago. Now Woodberry reached in his pocket, pulled out a handful of cards, and slapped them on the table. David riffled through them and his eyes lit up.

'It's Sobers. And Worrell. Terrific! Terrific!' He grabbed at Woodberry's hand and pumped it sincerely. 'You're a genius, Mr Woodberry.'

Woodberry blew a smoke-ring and leant over the counter conspiratorially.

'Tell me, David.'

'Yes.'

'How come you've gone a bit jungle-happy all of a sudden? I mean all those fellows are a bit on the dark side, aren't they? They weren't so hard to find because nobody wants them, if you get my drift.'

David thought for a minute.

'I've got all the English ones.'

'How about some Australians?' asked Woodberry. 'Or South Africans? Eh? They're a bit . . . sprucer . . . you get me?'

'No,' said David decisively. 'I want those ones for the moment, Mr W., if you don't mind.'

Woodberry gave a little smirk. 'Suit yourself.'

thirteen

Over the next few days, the West Indian players became a major feature of David's private games. Particularly Garry Sobers, the loose-limbed all-rounder who in his worldly incarnation was thrilling English cricket crowds with both bat and ball in the current test series. The fuss over the net seemed to die down and to David's regret and puzzlement all went quiet next door. In fact, Judy had been concentrating on getting used to her new school; her father had been working the afternoon shift and every hour of overtime he could get, to help cover the girls' boat trip and all the moving costs.

On this particular day, David as usual brought the Sobers card in at number three.

'OK, Sobers! You're in,' he said. 'It's a good pitch. This might be a record-breaker.'

Sobers grinned and waved at David. David rolled his pencil. There was a sharp click as Sobers hooked the ball elegantly to leg.

David pricked up his ears and looked to the window.

'Good strike, Judy. Your grandpa been teaching you well, man.' It was the big man's voice, drifting up from the garden. David turned to Sobers.

'Sorry, old chap, wait a mo.'

He ran to the window. Sobers, frowning, watched him go.

In the next-door net, Mr Samuels, still in his work overalls, tossed the ball down to Judy, the stroke-maker. She played it delicately, gracefully back. David watched, spellbound.

There was a harmony in the way father and daughter practised, an easy closeness and rhythm. It was as though both bat and ball were an extension of Dennis and Judy's bodies, something they had grown up with which had become an integral part of them. This was why the big man had been in such a hurry to get his net up: it was the way that he and Judy had been close in the past, and he wanted that closeness back again.

Sobers put his hands on hips and looked up to David impatiently. David was immersed in the game below him.

'Send me a spinner,' Judy said.

'Try this for size.'

The big man sent down a ball that Judy had to scramble to play away.

'Come right forward on them leg breaks,' he said. 'On the front foot. Kill the spin.'

He demonstrated the stroke to her. David remained totally engrossed.

Sobers folded his arms in bored exasperation.

* * *

The following day, and the day after, David's cards were virtually untouched. They remained arrayed in teams on the floor, but no game came to them. David's imagination had transferred itself to the flesh and blood action below. He was commentating in his best radio announcer voice, as Judy drove a ball into the netting.

'A great shot! Driving past silly mid-on. Well, they call him silly. But he isn't silly really. It's just what we say in cricket.'

David sat by the window, partly obscured by the curtain. He had appropriated Lillian's new hairbrush and was using it as a microphone. He entered two runs into the scorecard on his knee. His voice dropped to hushed awe.

'And that brings Sobers up to twenty-three. With his great bowling too, some people think that Garfield Sobers *is the greatest all-rounder the game has ever seen. And now he faces Wesley Hall again.'*

Judy squared up to face the next ball. The big man limbered up to bowl.

'No-one can match Wesley Hall for speed. This is a terrific contest.'

David's attention was distracted by Victor and Ruth, crossing on the stairs. David stopped his commentary to listen.

'I'm going back to the shop,' said Victor.

'Must you?' said Ruth. 'It's late.'

'I can get straight while it's quiet.'

Ruth fingered his lapel. 'You want to go out one night? A play or something. We could find a sitter.'

Victor stalled. 'Why start paying baby-sitters? Go yourself if you have to.'

He started to move on down the stairs. Ruth carried on up, despair in her eyes.

'Did you talk to the landlord?' he called after her.

She closed the door of the bedroom behind her. Victor shrugged and picked up his overcoat.

David returned loudly to his commentary. Judy was squaring up for the next ball.

'Sobers is still at the crease. Ready for anything Hall can throw at him, I dare say.' The big man had picked

up a bottle of beer and was taking a swig. He had put his hand inside his overalls and was absentmindedly but vigorously scratching. *'But Hall seems to have a little itch. I mean a little hitch. A big hitch.'*

Judy put her hands on her hips.

'The crowd is getting impatient.'

The big man retrieved his hand and prepared to bowl the next ball. David breathed a sigh of relief.

'Thank goodness that's over. Play has been resumed.' His voice dropped to a hush. *'Tension is mounting for the upcoming test . . .'*

As the evening wore on, 'Hall' and 'Sobers' extended the scope of their practice. Judy bowled for the big man to bat. And then they took turns to put on wicket-keeping gloves, throwing the ball harder and harder, testing one another's stretch and reflexes with more and more difficult balls.

Judy scuffed a catch. The ball fell to the floor, and she reached to pick it up. As she knelt down, a dark shadow passed over the setting sun. She glanced up. An apparition had appeared in the garden next door. She gasped.

It was a face. David's face. Staring at them from on top of an orange box in the middle of his garden lawn. He was in full cricket whites. They glowed in the evening gloom. His boots positively gleamed. The big man's jaw dropped.

'Judy,' he said. 'It's a professional. A real professional.'

David beamed.

'Hello,' Judy said.

'Hello.'

'You want to play?' she asked.

David nodded.

'Come and show us how it's done, young man,' said the big man.

David strode heroically towards them, eager to impress. His bat was tucked under his arm, his pads and gloves already on.

'Does your mother know you are here?' asked the big man, as he helped David scramble over the fence.

David mumbled, 'Uhuh.'

'Good,' said the big man. 'So what's your name, young fellow?'

'It's David, isn't it?' Judy said.

'Yes.'

The big man grinned. 'Was David killed the giant, wasn't it? Well now you can have a go at me. You met my daughter Judy. And me, you can call me Dennis.'

David looked up at him. 'Like the cricketer?'

'Like him, but a little different.' He guided David up towards the wicket. 'Now, take your bat and show us some sweet music. Here, Judy, take mid-off for me.'

Judy took up a position in the side netting, while David organised himself at the crease. He carefully found his middle, and squared up to face the ball.

Dennis gave the ball a ritual polish on his trouser-leg.

'Ready, David?'

David nodded. Dennis prepared to begin his run-up.

David held up his hand. Dennis stopped.

David knelt down and earnestly removed a scrap of mud from the pitch in front of him. Dennis raised his eyebrows at Judy. This boy meant business.

He tossed down a medium-paced ball. David stayed rooted to the spot. The ball rebounded off the back of the net. Judy tried to hide her smile.

'Takes a time to get your eye in, eh?' said Dennis. 'Here, try a slower one.'

The ball bounced gently in front of David. He made an ineffectual dab at it. It trickled into the net.

'Failing light. Failing light,' proffered Dennis. He

glanced dubiously at his daughter. 'Here, take the wicket for me, Judy.'

David faced the ball with undimmed eagerness.

'Tell you what,' said Dennis. 'I want you to take a good clean swing at this one. A nice clean swing.'

He lobbed down a slow ball. David curled his body up and then unleashed an almighty swipe. Judy ducked as David's follow-through narrowly missed her head. The ball rolled gently onto the stumps, and the bails toppled to the ground.

'Too bad. Too bad,' said Dennis sorrowfully. 'Maybe you're more of a bowling type. You want to try bowling?'

David nodded eagerly. 'Yes, please.'

Dennis tossed him the ball, and Judy picked up the bat. David paced out his run carefully. He spat on the ball and shined it vigorously on his trousers.

'Uh-oh! Look out, Judy!' warned Dennis. 'This young man has a mean streak on him.'

David grinned, despite himself. 'A real mean streak,' encouraged Dennis.

David trundled awkwardly down the pitch, and sent down a ball that went flying into the roof of the net, stayed poised there for a moment, and then dropped down almost vertically in front of Judy, who returned it gently down the pitch.

'Too much power,' said Dennis. 'Too much power. He can't control it yet.'

The next ball whizzed past Judy far too wide for her to reach. The one after that nearly hit Dennis at mid-off. Somehow the harder David tried, the more weird and wonderful became the balls he bowled. If they were near enough – and most were not – Judy played them effortlessly back to him.

David's final ball somehow flipped out of the back of his hand and went skying over the wall, narrowly missing the factory window beyond.

'Whoah!' said Dennis. 'Well done, sir. That's not bad, David. Not bad.' He beckoned Judy over.

'Tell me, David, they give you any coaching at that school of yours? A boy as keen as you.'

David looked uncomfortable. 'In a way.'

'What you mean, in a way?'

'They coach you if you are in the team.'

Dennis squatted on an old tea-chest.

'Winner takes all, is that the philosophy they teaching you?'

David shrugged his shoulders.

'Are you in the team?' asked Dennis.

David blushed. 'I'm scorer.'

'Scoring's a very good job, you know,' said Dennis. 'Very, very useful. But it's not the same as playin'. You want to play, right?'

'Yes,' whispered David.

'You want to be in that team.'

David hesitated.

'Say it, David,' insisted Dennis. 'After me! "I want to be in the team." Go on.'

David took a deep breath. 'I want to be in the team.'

'That's better,' said Dennis. 'Know what your goal is, you can reach it more easily.'

He turned to Judy. 'Right, sweetie?'

'Yes,' she said.

'What say we give him another try-out?'

A flutter of reluctance crossed her face.

'All right.'

'Sure?'

'Yes.'

Dennis turned back to David. 'You want to come again tomorrow?'

'Yes. Please.'

Dennis checked his watch. 'Let's see. What's my shift? Tomorrow we start a bit earlier. You don't have to wear full kit . . .'

David's face dropped.

'. . . if you don't want to.'

Dennis hoicked David back over the fence. 'See you tomorrow,' Judy said.

Ruth was calling from inside the house.

'David! David! Where are you?'

David stepped inside the kitchen door.

'Wondrous!' he said to himself. 'Wondrous oblivion.'

fourteen

The next day David was a man in a hurry. He dived off the train and dashed along the platform. He took the steps three at a time, dodging around the other passengers, and pushed his way to the ticket inspector. He managed to hook the strap of the satchel over the post at the ticket barrier, and almost pulled it over. Then he charged up the slope out of the station, flying past the newspaper vendor. 'England level series. Read all about it.' Down three streets, round three corners. And he was home.

At the Samuels' house a lilting rock-steady melody emanated from the open window of Loretta's bedroom.

Dennis and Judy were tapping the stumps into place in the garden. They looked up. David was in full kit once more, waiting expectantly on the other side of the fence.

Dennis lifted him over.

'Tomorrow come the easy way,' he said. 'Through the front. You going to do me an injury one of these days.'

He threw the ball to Judy. 'OK, young woman,' he said. 'I want 'em all straight. Straight and steady.' He placed a leaf on the ground about three-quarters of the way down the pitch. 'On this spot here. Exactly.'

He turned to David. 'OK, now, Mr Wiseman, sir, you take the bat. Just play this one defensively, and I'm going to watch your action.' Judy threw it down exactly as prescribed, dead on target. David tried to play it, and missed. He looked helplessly up at Dennis. Dennis stepped behind David and enfolded him with his huge body. He grasped the bat over David's hands, and prepared to make the stroke with him.

'Good. Yes. Head up and watch the ball.'

Dennis and David together blocked the ball successfully, and sent it back down to Judy. Other balls followed in steady succession. David was in heaven. The big man was holding him firmly, and they were hitting every ball. Gradually the rhythm of the movement took him over.

'Good. Good, man. You getting the feel?' asked Dennis.

'Yes. I am.'

'You making a big face on this bat, see. Like a big

smile, and you say to yourself. "No-one can walk past me." '

'No-one can walk past me.'

'Now I leave go, you can do it yourself.'

Dennis gradually released his grip and stepped back. David successfully blocked the next balls on his own. A leap of excitement reverberated inside him. He was getting it. His body was getting it. On its own.

The balls came down, steady, repetitive. He felt himself to be a machine, well-oiled, blocking every one.

'Great,' said Dennis. 'That's great, man. You playing like Trevor Bailey already. Genius.'

Suddenly Judy sent down a ball that fizzed unexpectedly off the turf. It skimmed past the wicket and slammed into the back netting.

'Whoah, Judy!' called Dennis. 'Easy now.'

'Good ball!' called out David, once he'd recovered from his shock. Judy ignored him.

Dennis ambled over to her. 'What's up, girl?'

Judy shrugged her shoulders and scowled.

Dennis called back to David. 'Don't worry, David. She just got me back and I reckon now she don't want to share me.'

He put an arm around his daughter. 'Didn't I tell you last night there's more than enough of me to go round,' he murmured to her, patting his stomach. She looked at him without expression. 'And you need a friend your own age anyway. Mmm?'

Judy ventured a tiny smile.

'My Judy.' Dennis said. 'My special girl.' It was true. For Dennis the primary purpose of the net had been as a way of reconnecting with his beloved middle daughter after these hard years of absence. Cricket had always been what connected them in the past, and his hope had been that it would be what would bring them close in the present. He held her tighter.

Judy's smile grew. 'Better?' he asked. She nodded. 'You want to play now?'

Judy held her hand out to take the ball. Dennis flicked his wrist, and winked.

Judy gave the leather a good shine on her dress. The next ball she sent down had some spin in it, a leg break. It hit the pitch at the usual place. But it went in a different direction. David played the same stroke, and missed.

'Oops!' said Dennis. 'Here we have a problem, Mr Bailey. She ain't always going to serve it up so convenient. This one was spinning. You got to have a different stroke. One for every kind of ball. But since you got one already you can practise, it's time I got some liquid refreshment down me. All right, Judy?'

He waved a departing hand and disappeared into the house.

David continued to practise the stroke.

Judy looked David up and down. He gave up and stood awkwardly, swinging his bat.

'How come you so keen on cricket?' Judy asked.

David shrugged.

'Don't your father teach you?'

'My dad doesn't play cricket,' answered David. 'They don't play it where he comes from. Anyway, he's got the shop.'

They stood in awkward silence.

'I'll show you my cricket cards one day,' volunteered David. 'I've got hundreds. I've got a bat signed by the whole Surrey team.'

'Surrey? Who is Surrey?'

'It's a team.'

'Is it a big team?'

'It's the best team. In England. Surrey and Yorkshire. And Middlesex. They are the best.'

They moved closer. Judy leant nonchalantly against a post, still eyeing him up and down.

'You want to bowl?'

'OK. Just a minute . . .'

He sank to the ground and started to unbuckle his pads. Judy watched him.

'I didn't see my dad for nearly four years,' she said, as if to explain her behaviour earlier. 'My mum came to visit, once.'

'Who looked after you?' asked David, perturbed.

'My grandma of course.'

'Where is she now?'

'Back home. In Barbados.'

David shook his head. 'I haven't got a grandma.'

Judy squatted down to face him. 'How come?'

'I'm not sure exactly. They all got killed in the war.'

'That's terrible.'

'No it's not,' said David. 'I never knew them. Dad says you don't miss what you never had.'

'You wouldn't have to know them to miss them,' insisted Judy. 'It doesn't stop you, does it, missing them?'

David went silent while he pondered this thought.

Dennis emerged from the kitchen, and stood watching the children talking. He couldn't help being touched to see his daughter making a friend in the neighbourhood. It had been such a hard road to get to this point. Doors slammed in their faces. Sign after sign in the windows that said TO LET: NO COLOURED. All they had wanted was to get out of that leaky attic and have enough space to bring their children to. It had taken months of searching but thankfully in the end they had found a decent landlord who could see that they were both in work, steady jobs, and would pay the rent.

Not that his job in the foundry was anything to write home about. It was dirty and dangerous. But at least it was secure. In Barbados he had been a proper engineer, maintaining the machinery on a cotton plantation. Nobody would give him a job like that here, though they'd been glad enough to employ Grace as a nurse. Four years it had taken and now they were set up.

What a horrible welcome they'd had to this street, the horseshit on the doorstep the first day, the neighbours' whispers and glances! But here was David, the giant-killer, come to play, and befriending his daughter. He sighed and checked his watch.

'Children!' he called. 'We have to pack up now. Judy, time to do some homework.'

Judy pulled at the stumps. David picked up the bails.

'Do you like it here?' he asked.

She eyed David uncertainly. 'Maybe!' she said.

Dennis heaved David back over the fence. 'Tomorrow we do a bit of bowling,' he said.

As he set David down he looked up to see Ruth across the fence, arms akimbo, eyes on fire.

'Go inside,' she ordered David.

Then she stood there, lost for words.

'How do you do?' said Dennis affably. 'Your son is a raw talent. But he need a little shaping up yet.'

'Yes.'

The big man reached out a hand over the fence.

'Dennis.'

Ruth shook it stiffly.

'Ruth.'

'And you've met my daughter Judy. Anytime your son wants to come over and practise he just knock on the door.'

'Thank you very much,' said Ruth, disarmed. She turned sharply away and strode back into the house.

David was fetching himself a glass of milk from the fridge. Ruth banged the door behind her.

'So?'

David looked at the ground.

'Mr Samuels is coaching me. He says I need proper coaching.'

'And?'

'Judy's grandpa used to play for Barbados. Everybody plays cricket over there. Even the girls.'

'Did anybody give you permission to play next door? Did you ask your father about it?'

David shook his head. 'They are very nice, Mum. They gave me a bit of a mango. It's like a pear. Or a melon. It was funny.'

Ruth's fury and anxiety were all mixed up. 'Don't give me about mangoes. You'll get us into trouble!'

David gave up trying to schmooze his mother. He walked disconsolately up the hallway, dragging his bat behind him. Ruth wrestled with her difficulty in disappointing him. That damned Mrs Wilson or her spies saw everything. This was a line she and Victor had drawn. For good reason. For David's own good. For the good standing of the family. Yet . . .

David trudged heavily up the stairs. Ruth called after him.

'Next time you ask first. Understand?'

'Yes, Mum! YES, MUM!'

He bounded excitedly up the stairs. Ruth realised to her dismay that she had given in to him. 'But you are not to go in the house,' she called. 'You stay in the garden.' Her voice tailed away. 'Maybe Daddy won't mind if you stay in the garden.'

fifteen

Daddy did mind. That weekend Victor watched what had become a daily session from David's bedroom window. The three cricket fanatics were in the net. David had the bat, and Dennis had his arms around him again, demonstrating a sweeping cover drive. Victor didn't like this man he didn't know being so close to his son. It made him uncomfortable. And such a stupid game! But he couldn't stop it now. Ruth had given way, as usual. He just had to hope his son would get over it.

A sweating Grace emerged from the kitchen carrying a tray of drinks.

'Come and get your colas,' she called. 'You entitled to a break.'

Dennis called back. 'I'm entitled to something a little stronger, Mrs Samuels.'

He headed towards the kitchen.

'You ain't entitled to nothing,' replied Grace.

Judy, Dorothy and David came eagerly over to pick up their drinks. Grace looked David in the eye. 'So, David, you is a Jewish boy?'

David nodded diffidently, sipping his fizzy drink.

'Judy told us about your granpa 'n' granma,' continued Grace. 'You see, girls, we got a real live Jewish boy here. Same as Jesus.'

Judy and Dorothy peered wide-eyed at David over the tops of their cola-bottles.

'Me never met a Jew before,' said Judy.

David fumbled his bat nervously.

'The people of the bible, girl,' said Grace. 'These people gave us the Old Testament, from Genesis to Ruth. These are God's chosen people.'

David realised the interrogation wasn't hostile. He beamed from ear to ear. He had never felt chosen before. At school being Jewish was worthy of insult or at best indifference.

Dennis returned from the kitchen with his bottle of beer. 'A boy is a boy, Grace. An' a boy got to learn how to play cricket.' He turned to David. 'Ain't that right?'

Grace was not to be deflected. She had extra reasons for making David feel welcome. Survival in this neighbourhood, that might be one good reason. 'This is a special boy,' she said. 'David, we are glad to have you here.'

sixteen

The following Tuesday was a horrid day. Tuesday was one of the days that Ruth worked in the drapery. David joined her at the shop after school, and walked back home with her when business began to slacken. As they rounded the corner shop to enter Duchess Road, Mrs Wilson and Mrs Dunkley were standing talking on the street ahead. A young man was with them, wiry with pretty-boy good looks. He was first to catch sight of Ruth and David. He nudged Mrs Wilson. As Ruth and David approached, Mrs Wilson spat hard into the gutter at Ruth's feet and then pointedly moved away across the street.

Ruth recoiled with shock. She couldn't believe it. This was like when she was a child in Nazi Germany. She pushed David away up the street.

Mrs Dunkley eyed her with folded arms. Ruth struggled to control her panic.

'Good afternoon, Mrs Dunkley,' she said.

'Mrs Wiseman.'

'Anything the matter, Mrs Dunkley?' asked Ruth.

Mrs Dunkley's tone was acid. 'We were just

noticing how friendly your son is with the new arrivals, Mrs Wiseman.'

'I haven't encouraged it, Mrs Dunkley.'

'You haven't stopped it neither, my dear.'

Ruth fought to hold back her tears. 'I also am an immigrant, Mrs Dunkley,' she said. 'Should I teach my son to despise immigrants?'

Mrs Dunkley spluttered. 'Don't upset yourself, Mrs Wiseman. Not all immigrants are the same, I'm sure.' She glimpsed Mrs Wilson eyeing her meaningfully from across the road. 'Must be off. I'm sorry to bother you.'

'No bother, Mrs Dunkley,' replied Ruth. 'No bother.'

She collected David from further up the street and they walked on, heads down. Approaching the house, Ruth looked up with a gasp to see the pretty-boy standing at their gatepost. With a mirthless smirk and a bow he opened the gate for them. Ruth turned to face him as she closed the gate behind her. He smiled sweetly. Ruth shuddered.

* * *

A worried Ruth had insisted that David come by the shop the following day after school. He sat restlessly at the counter, catching up on the cricket news in his father's evening paper. Ruth was gathering up short ends of material for the next cushion-making session. Victor harangued a supplier on the telephone.

'Since when was Tuesday Friday? This is a piece of magic I can do without.'

David put down the paper and stood up.

'Yes, I know you do your best,' Victor muttered and put the phone down.

David timidly approached the back office. 'Can I go home, Dad?'

'As long as your mother is in the shop you stay here.'

'Mr Samuels will be there,' insisted David. 'He's on earlies today.'

'And when are you going to do your homework?' exploded Victor. 'I don't see you doing any homework these days. You go to a good school. You want to become a schlump who's no good for anything but working in a factory? Like Samuels, on "earlies". Or running a shop like this every hour of day or night? Fawning at stupid customers who bring back mangled goods and want a refund, they think you can't refuse them.'

David stood silenced. Tears glistened in his eyes. He sat down and began to fumble with his satchel. Further up the shop Ruth addressed a new customer.

'Good afternoon. Can I help you?'

'I'd like to look at some curtain material. Blue.'

The presence of a customer brought Victor back to earth. He tapped his pencil on his order book.

'All right,' he said eventually to his son. 'Go. But come back if he isn't there. I don't want you to stay in the house on your own.'

David slung his satchel over his shoulder. 'I do my homework every day, Dad. Honestly, I do.'

'If you say so. Now go.'

David tore out of the shop and pummelled down the street.

* * *

A bouncing cricket calypso rang out on Loretta's gramophone. Judy and her father were already practising in the net when David dashed into the back garden.

'Come on, young man,' called Dennis. 'You're late. Get your kit on.'

David reappeared a moment later. He clambered over the fence with practised ease. For the first time he had compromised and dispensed with full cricket gear.

Dennis raised his eyebrows. 'All right now, let's see you running through some of these strokes we've been laying down here. Judy, get behind the wicket. We'll see if this young man remember anything.'

David took the bat. Dennis sent down a series of balls in rapid succession, calling out the stroke that he wanted David to play.

'Forward block now . . . good, man!

'Cover drive . . . excellent!

'This one, step and cut . . . but it's a winner, man.'

Dennis shouted continual encouragement. In the warmth of his approval, David was already an altogether different player from the one who had first stepped over the fence a few weeks ago. Most balls he hit. Sometimes his dreaminess got the better of him. Judy snapped up the ones he missed and whipped them back to her father. But he didn't let them bother him. He was beginning to have a confidence, an ease in his body, that had been entirely lacking before.

David's sureness grew in the following fortnight. Come rain or shine, the net was in use every day of the week. Ruth watched his progress – and his antics

– with a mixture of anxiety, pride and amusement. The fuss with the neighbours seemed to have subsided. She kept a safe distance from Mrs Wilson, and began to hope that the worst had passed. Eventually she set aside her misgivings, and gave David a tray of drinks to take over to Dennis and the girls. She thoughtfully put a glass of beer amidst the orange squash. Dennis was grateful, but she found herself shy in the big man's presence and kept a distance.

Once when Dennis was on afternoon shift, David and Judy took it on themselves to start coaching little Dorothy, who proved a willing learner. Another time they found themselves at catching practice in the pouring rain. Rather than go in, they continued in their raincoats. Then Dennis focused for a while on David's bowling action. The great day came when David actually bowled out Judy, who at first pretended she hadn't been trying, but in the end congratulated him on the delivery.

Dennis was packing away the pads and stumps at the end of practice. Ruth called to him nervously over the fence.

'I'm very grateful.'

'Oh, it's not a problem, Mrs Wiseman.' He looked up at her. 'You OK? You look like the roof has fallen in.'

'Do I?' she said. 'I'm sorry.'

'No it's . . .'

'Would you like a cup of tea?' Ruth blurted out.

'Tea?' replied Dennis uncertainly. 'Sure. Whatever you have is fine.'

He sat quietly at the kitchen table, while Ruth busied herself with the cups and saucers. David and Judy squatted in the sunshine on the back step. David was showing her his treasures. First the box of cricket cards.

'Four hundred and thirty-seven,' said David. 'All different. Not counting swaps.'

Judy looked mystified. Why would anyone want pictures of cricketers, when there was a real game to be played?

Ruth took off her apron and joined Dennis at the table.

'Hey!' said Dennis. 'You looking pretty now. Like a young girl. Too young to have these children.'

Ruth blushed. 'I married very young.'

'Well your husband was very smart. He snapped

you up quick before someone else could get hold of you.'

Ruth smiled and passed Dennis his tea.

David picked up his next treasure. 'This is the bat I told you about.'

Judy took hold of it, and tried it out for weight and balance.

'No, no!' said David. 'You can't use it.'

'How come?' said Judy. 'It seem good to me.'

'You'd ruin the autographs.'

Judy shook her head in bafflement.

Meanwhile Ruth was telling Dennis a story. 'We spent three hours after supper making cushions. We did a lot of . . . not pillow talk, we do cushion talk.'

Dennis laughed heartily.

David passed Judy his scorebooks. Judy thumbed through them wonderingly, the mass of tiny writing, dots and statistics.

'Every county and test match for the past three years,' declared David proudly.

'You too brainy for cricket,' said Judy.

'No, I'm not. Anyway, you have to be brainy in modern cricket. I read it in an article, about tactics. That's why Cowdrey is captain. There's other batters as good. But he's got the brains.'

'How you know?' asked Judy.

'From his accent and everything,' replied David. 'You can tell he went to university.'

Judy frowned.

At the table, Dennis's attentiveness was beginning to move Ruth. She never normally confided in anyone the way she was confiding in him. Talking about her life with Victor was touching a raw nerve.

'We stuff a lot . . . we stuff a lot of cushions,' she said. Her eyes filled with tears.

'Oh, golly, Ruth!' Dennis exclaimed consolingly.

It was dark and a little misty by the time Victor got home. Thursdays was late closing, and he'd stayed to tidy up after shutting the shop. He walked up the street carrying his cardboard box of accounts books, and put his key in the lock. On the mat was a cheap blue envelope. He bent down to pick it up.

The house was quiet. The family were already in bed. Ruth had left his dinner on the kitchen table, cold by now. He couldn't be bothered to warm it up. He lifted off the lid and hungrily snatched a few mouthfuls. He opened the envelope. The message was scrawled in large capitals. GET RID OF THE DARKIES. He spat his food back on the plate.

seventeen

The rain teemed onto the pitch and onto David, at his usual place steadfastly watching over the scoreboard. The other boys were sheltering forlornly under a tree. The rainwater was beginning to drip through the leaves. They shivered and stamped their feet. Mr Pugh under his brolly pulled out his pipe. David could feel the rain dripping off his nose.

'Sir!' he said.

Mr Pugh looked down at him.

'Oh I doubt if we'll be playing again today, Wiseman,' he said, swivelling his brolly.

'No, sir,' said David. The rain poured off Mr Pugh's umbrella and down David's neck.

'Sir!' said David.

'Yes, boy.'

'I don't want to score any more after today, please, sir.'

'What's the matter, Wiseman? I thought you liked scoring.'

'I do, sir, but I'd like to play now.'

Mr Pugh scowled. 'Would you, indeed?'

He fixed his eye threateningly on David. 'Nuisance halfway through the season.'

David met his gaze. Pugh puffed vainly on his pipe.

'Oh, all right.'

'Thank you, sir.'

'Look on the notice-board on Tuesday.'

'Yes, sir.' The downpour intensified. David smiled.

'Let's not get wet, boys!' shouted Mr Pugh. 'Call it a draw. Three cheers for the St. Dunstan's firsts. Hip hip hooray. Hip hip whatever.'

The boys charged off for the changing rooms through a sheet of rain.

'Hip hip hooray. Hip hip hooray. Hip hip hooray.'

* * *

Water was everywhere. It spattered on the pavement. It poured onto roofs, along gutters, down pipes. It gushed into drains. It soaked into the hungry earth. And it spurted from the back of Ruth's new washing machine, forming an ever-expanding puddle on the floor. Ruth vainly tried to swab it up but the puddle grew remorselessly. She pulled the machine away from the wall and tried to bind up the leak with a towel. Water sprayed all over her, but she succeeded in slowing the flood.

The front door banged. A rain-soaked David hurtled into the room, brimming with excitement.

'Mum! I've got some news.'

'David! Thank goodness you're here. Go and get help. Quickly! Quickly!'

David plunged back out into the downpour, beetled across the front gardens and banged the next-door knocker.

Dennis answered the door, dressed in a white singlet. On nights, he'd only just got up.

'David, come in, man.'

'No, Dennis. Come quickly. We've got an emergency.'

Dennis grabbed his bag of tools and followed David at a trot back across the front gardens. They scurried into the kitchen. David watched from the safety of the doorway.

'I've got some news, Dennis.'

'Jus a minute, David.'

He sized up the situation. 'This is a washing machine?'

'For washing clothes,' replied Ruth from down behind the machine. 'Victor bought it. I've hardly even used it yet.'

Dennis pulled the washing machine further out

from the wall, so that there was room for both he and Ruth to get down behind it. He unbound the towel and handed it to her. Water spurted out.

'David, pass my tool-bag,' he said.

David did as he was bidden. Dennis reached in and pulled out a wrench. Ruth watched as he worked at the connector. 'This is the problem here. It's cross-threaded. A lot of pressure. Man who connected this should have screwed his own head on first.' The hose finally came away. Dennis picked up the gushing hose end and forced it back onto the connector. A fine spray flew up, drenching himself and Ruth.

'Ruth. Give me a hand here.' He took her hand in his and guided it onto the hose end.

'Hold it tight, nice and tight while I fasten it up. Watch yourself.'

They crouched down side by side while he reached for the wrench and expertly fastened on the hose. Ruth watched him, in fear and wonder. She could feel the touch of him close to her through her thin, wet dress.

It was done. Dennis let the wrench drop. Ruth stepped quickly away. David clapped.

'Wondrous, Dennis.'

'Thank you so much,' said Ruth. 'I was completely ... it was terrible. Look at my floor.'

Dennis laughed. He reached for the sodden towel.

'You mop. I'll use this one. It won't take a minute. David, go and get dry.'

Dennis and Ruth wrung and squeezed in easy harmony. The rain stopped and the sun came peeping through. They opened the kitchen door and windows to let the air through. The pool on the floor began to subside. The drips in the windows glowed in the sunlight.

They knelt together over the bucket. Dennis turned to Ruth.

'Would David like to come to a charity do on Saturday? A couple of our cricketers is going to be there signing autographs.'

'I'm not sure,' replied Ruth. 'On his own?'

'You come too,' said Dennis. 'Why not? And Victor too.'

'Victor!' said Ruth.

'Sure.'

'I don't expect so. I'll ask him.'

'He puts in some long hours, your husband.'

Ruth nodded resignedly and turned back to her mop.

'You and David then,' suggested Dennis. 'And Judy. Mrs Samuels is working nights this weekend. So I would have the honour to be your escort.' He bowed graciously.

'Yes,' said Ruth excitedly.

'Good, good.'

She met his eyes for a moment, and looked away hastily.

'No, Dennis,' she said. 'I couldn't.'

David came charging back in his dry clothes, unable to hold onto his news a moment longer.

'Mum. I'm stopping scoring. I'm going to play on Thursday. Dennis.'

He grinned broadly. Dennis rose off the floor to pump his hand.

'David, good man, David. Now you show 'em what you made of.'

Ruth squeezed her mop fiercely, trying to stop the churning inside. Dennis lifted David high off the floor.

'Saturday you're going to meet some true gods of the game,' he said. He looked over to Ruth. 'Maybe.'

eighteen

The day of David's much-anticipated return to the cricket pitch came quickly. It was a scratch game presided over by the deaf and aging umpire, Mr Robinson. The players were a motley bunch, the overweight and under-fit, the indifferent and the un-motivated. Their kit was ill-fitting and sometimes missing altogether.

David was in whites and pads and facing the wayward bowling with unusual seriousness. He had come in late in the innings when his team looked like going down to an early loss. Now he played carefully and defensively, blocking the ball in a classic stance. The wicket-keeper, Fox, a big boy with trousers slipping off his belly, had been one of Bloom's persecutors at that incident with the desks some weeks ago.

'Hurry up and get out, Wiseman,' he muttered as David squared up to face the next ball. 'We want to go home.'

David took no notice. He hit the ball for a careful single, thus keeping the batting, since it was the end of the over and the bowling team were changing ends. The scoreboard showed his team fifty runs behind. The remainder of David's team waited glumly at the edge of the pitch.

One boy, Baxter, yelled out to Mr Robinson, 'Can we go and get changed, sir?'

'Got to support your last man, Baxter,' called back Mr Robinson. 'Don't you want to know if you've won or lost?'

'No, sir.'

Mr Robinson shook his head sorrowfully and turned down his hearing aid.

Despite the lack of support, David appeared immovable. It wasn't a glamorous innings. The score crept up slowly in ones and twos. Rarely did David really let swing. He was slow and deliberate. But he managed to keep the batting, was defensively totally sound and very effective. The scoreboard showed the margin only nine. The waiting boys began to heckle.

'What's wrong with him?'

'Wiseman is on drugs.'

'He's super-boy.'

'It's not natural.'

David went for another determined single. Even Mr Robinson began to lose patience.

'Good grief, Wiseman, it's only a game.'

'Get rid of him, sir,' said Fox. 'He's spoiling it for everybody.'

Stung by the comments, David took a suicidal swing at the next ball, and was bowled out. The watching crowd gave a cheer of relief.

Mr Robinson accosted David as he left the pitch. 'That was very good, Wiseman. Only eight runs short of victory. I'll tell Mr Pugh to give you a proper game.'

'Thank you, sir,' said David. 'I want to be in the team.'

'I'm sure you do,' replied Mr Robinson wonderingly.

David grinned, shouldered his bat, and strode towards the pavilion.

nineteen

Grace had organised for David to come over and give what she called 'a lickle demonstration'. He stood awkwardly in the middle of the living room, a battered blue prayer book in his hand. Grace slipped out of the door.

'OK, David? Jus' wait here one moment.'

The sun streamed through the net curtains. Judy sat awkwardly on the battered settee, beside the grey-haired Mrs Jackson, a stalwart of Grace's church, looking severe and formal in her Sunday suit. David shifted uneasily from one foot to another, and looked around him. Multi-coloured cushions were scattered everywhere. And bright-coloured plastic flowers in coloured vases. Photos of the family adorned the walls and mantelpiece. There was one of Judy's grandad in full cricket gear, holding a trophy; there was Dennis and Grace's wedding picture; and one of Dennis as a young man in his army uniform – he too had signed up to fight for the Empire in its hour of need.

Grace shouted up the stairs, 'Loretta! Dorothy!'

She bustled along the corridor. 'Mr Samuels. Mr Johnson. Mrs Jackson waiting!'

David could hear Dennis in the kitchen. 'Mrs Jackson? I thought it was David. It's not a prayer meeting, is it, Grace?' Dennis didn't share his wife's thirst for organised religion.

'It's just David. Now come and listen. Listen and learn.'

Grace and the family filed into the room, Dennis bringing up the rear. They sat down, Dorothy on Dennis's lap. Grace motioned to David.

'We ready.'

David put his skullcap on his head. Grace whispered to Dennis next to her, 'Where's your hat.'

He began to get up again. 'I left it in the—'

Grace pushed him back down. 'You have no time for that.' She fished a frilly lace handkerchief from her sleeve. 'Here, put this on.'

Dennis put the hanky on his head and motioned to Mr Johnson. Mr Johnson hastily covered his head with his trilby. David opened his prayer book. The family settled back into their seats. David began to chant melodiously in Hebrew.

'Shalom aleichem, malachei hasharet, malachei elyon, melech malchei hamlachim hakadosh baruch hu.'

Dorothy looked puzzled. 'He's reading backwards,' she whispered to Loretta.

'That's how they do it.'

'Shhh,' said their father.

David faltered for a moment. His eyes lifted from the page, and met Judy's. She smiled encouragement at him. He returned to his singing, the ancient tunes ringing out in his young boy's voice.

'Boachem lashalom, malachei hashalom, malachei elyon, melech malchei hamlachim hakadosh baruch hu.'

The family listened in respectful silence. Dennis closed his eyes. There was a holy feeling in the air, as the sun slanted through the net curtains and onto the bright cushions and cloths. David completed the melody, and warm silence hovered around them.

Then the family broke into enthusiastic applause.

'Beautiful,' said Grace. 'Truly beautiful! Mrs Jackson, what say we ask David to give a presentation at Sunday School prize day?'

'David,' said Mrs Jackson. 'We would be truly honoured.'

Judy pulled a dubious face.

David and Judy burst excitedly into the Wiseman kitchen.

'Mum,' called out David. 'Can I show Judy a beigel? She doesn't know what a beigel . . . is.'

David ground to a halt. Ruth and Victor were stood at the far end of the kitchen looking daggers at one another.

'What's the matter?' David asked.

'Nothing,' said Victor.

'I bought a dress,' said Ruth. 'Not an expensive dress. A cheap dress. A special offer.'

'It's all right,' said Victor. 'Not a problem. You bought a dress.' He hated to be shown up in front of Judy.

'You want me to take it back?' said Ruth. 'If you want, I'll take it back.'

Victor shook his head.

twenty

Ruth had been right about Victor. He didn't want to go to the charity benefit. It was on a Saturday, a shop day. The busiest day. He didn't want to leave the shop early and then have to pay extra staff to be there, even if he could trust them, which he couldn't. And neither cricket nor socials were his cup of tea. He was happy for Ruth and David to go. At least he'd said he was happy. But then he'd kicked up a fuss about the dress. Ruth didn't know if it was to do with the money or for some other reason, but it made her cross. While she had been apprehensive about going before, she was determined to have a good time now.

The social was at a restaurant in Notting Hill. They took the tube to Notting Hill Gate, and then walked. Ruth saw a lot of black people on the street in this part of town, West Indians, more than they ever saw in South London. Soon they were in a line of snazzy dressers queuing at the entrance. She and David were the only whites in the line and it made her nervous. She was glad she had the new dress and some earrings and that she'd spent a bit of time on her make-up. David had been bowled over when he saw her. He couldn't remember ever seeing his mother look so . . . so glamorous.

A sharp-suited Dennis insisted on paying. They could hear the thump of a band. The sign at the ticket desk said: Benefit for West Indian Standing Conference – Personal Appearances Frank Worrell Gary Sobers, Live ska music. Before they knew it Dennis was leading them up the stairs and into the fray. The music got louder.

'Nice dress, Ruth,' Dennis said. 'You look nervous. Are you all right?'

'I'm fine,' Ruth said. But she was pale as a sheet.

'Judy, make sure you save me one dance now.'

In what was normally the restaurant area, the two cricketers, Garry Sobers and Frank Worrell, both in their West Indies team blazers, were surrounded by a worshipping crowd. They were signing autographs and reminiscing with the assembled company.

David and Judy followed Dennis into the room. David's eyes practically popped out of his head as Frank Worrell spotted Dennis and waved.

'Hey, Dennis!'

'How you do, Frank?'

'My father sends his best to you.'

'Yes, man.'

Dennis pushed David and Judy forward.

'Look, I have two youngsters here want to listen to your chat and gossip.'

'Send them up. Send them up.'

'Go on, children. Don't be shy.'

Judy and David, eyes shining, joined the line for autographs.

Dennis bent to Ruth's ear. 'Two of the best cricketers in the world there, man.'

He led her into the back room, where there was a dance floor and a bar. Ruth was hit by a wave of energy. The band was blasting out a ska number. The floor was already jumping, couples jiving and twisting, swivelling their hips, a group of men jiggling and sliding their feet in a dance Dennis later told her was a shuffle. Ruth was terrified but also excited, buzzing, hungry for experience. Dennis greeted old friends, introduced them to his new neighbour, and went to fetch her a drink. She soaked up the atmosphere.

Dennis returned with the drinks.

'I want this dance, man,' he said. 'I want this dance right now.'

'I can't,' she said. 'No, Dennis.'

'All right,' said Dennis. 'Let's sit down for a while and watch. See. It's not so hard.'

They perched on a couple of chairs at the edge of the dance floor. 'Cheers!' Dennis said to her, and they clinked glasses. She gulped at her drink.

Go home, bad-minded woman go home
Go home, leave my business alone
You've been talking all day
You never kneel and pray

Ruth rejected all Dennis's attempts to get her to dance. But she was happy to let him go off and dance himself. She jigged up and down happily watching the dancing. People were kind and hospitable and keen to buy her drinks. She was keen to drink them. She was having a lovely time.

After a while she thought she should go back to check on Judy and David. She was a little wobbly walking down the corridor, but she found them without difficulty. They were rapt listening to the cricket talk. Garry was in the middle of some convoluted story about an innings he played in last year's test series in Australia. They were fine. She returned to her usual spot at the edge of the dance floor.

A skinny and vivacious black woman, Charlene, grabbed her by the hand. 'Come on! Dance!'

She pulled Ruth onto the floor.

'I can't.'

'Of course you can. Follow me.'

Ruth gave in. She bobbed and skitted about to the music, imitating Charlene. It was a fast number, with a pumping beat.

'That's it, you getting it now! Just move your hips like so . . .'

Ruth began to swivel her hips, the drink fuelling her, all inhibition beginning to fall away.

'If my husband could see me now!' she cried.

'He would be proud of you, darling,' yelled Charlene.

Dennis caught sight of Ruth on the floor and came over, protesting.

'You say you won't dance with me and now I catch you with this lady.' He clapped his hands and joined in excitedly with Ruth and Charlene. 'I catch you all right!' The saxophone started to blow hot and the three of them swivelled and shook in unison, laughing with delight and joy.

'Yes, dance, man!'

'I'm getting it.'

'Show me the moves, now, show me the moves . . .'

The song came to an end. Ruth clapped excitedly and poured back her drink. A slow ballad began, rock-steady.

I'm in a dancing mood
I'm in a dancing mood
I'm in a dancing mood

Dennis recognised the tune. 'Come on,' he said to Ruth. 'I want this dance.'

He took her in his big arms. They began to slow jive together, Dennis leading Ruth through the turns. She gradually let go her anxiety, and allowed herself to go with him. She blinked open her eyes and looked at her hand in his hand. One white, one black. It didn't mean anything, did it? All that fear. What for?

When you feel the beat
You've got to move your feet
You've got to clap your hands
You've got all the soul
Deep inside
That you can't hide

Ruth realised that Dennis was talking to her, but she couldn't hear anything he was saying. She closed her eyes, and leant into his body.

'See that guy over there, the guy in the cream suit,' Dennis was saying, pointing to an elderly black man in amongst a little group of bearded and sandalled whites. 'He's a poet, you know, one of the best we got . . . hey, you aren't even looking! I give up. I give up.'

Ruth smiled. She kept her eyes shut. She snuggled closer to him. He turned her around so her back was to him, and wrapped his arms around her.

David and Judy peered round the entrance. Judy did a little shimmy to the music. David caught sight of Dennis enfolding his mother.

'Look, Judy. Dennis is teaching her how to bat.'

Judy threw a sceptical glance at the adults, and yanked David back towards the other room.

'Does your mum play cricket too?' asked David as he tumbled after her.

Ruth swivelled round in Dennis's arms and pulled him in tight to her. The saxophone wailed.

'Whoa, sister!' said Dennis, gently loosening the embrace. He took her hand in his, waltz-style. 'Like this. Like this.'

I'm in a dancing mood
I'm in a dancing mood
I'm in a dancing mood
She pressed in close to him.

* * *

The phone rang in the near-dark hallway of the Wiseman house. Victor picked it up. 'Mrs Simmonds! I'm just back from the shop. I'll come and pick up Lillian.'

The letter-box flapped open and a familiar blue envelope dropped onto the mat.

'Just a minute, Mrs Simmonds.'

Victor dropped the phone, dashed for the door and yanked it open. He looked up and down the street. Mr Cartwright was digging his front garden. Apart from that, nothing. No-one. He stood listening, poised on the step.

Mrs Simmonds plaintive voice emerged from the dangling phone. *'Hello? Mr Wiseman? Mr Wiseman?'*

Victor slowly closed the door behind him. He heard a rustle in Mrs Dunkley's hedge two doors down. He leapt across the gardens and dived over the hedge. He landed in a freshly dug flower bed. A tabby-cat yowled and dashed away.

A young man's scampering feet rounded the corner by the tobacconist's.

'*Mr Wiseman?*' said the telephone. '*Are you still there, Mr Wiseman?*'

Victor cursed.

twenty-one

A number of the first team were clustered round the cricket notice-board. They were in ebullient mood. Pritchard began to chant. *'We're going to win the cup. We're going to win the cup. Ee-aye-addio. We're going to win the cup.'*

David pushed his way through them. 'Are the teams up?'

They ignored him, caught up in their own brilliance. Jessop burst into song as they sauntered away. *'There was Reece, Reece, batting at the crease . . .'*

The others joined in. *'In the stores, in the stores.'*

David scanned the notice-board eagerly. The teams were listed for a practice game, first versus second team. David's finger tracked down the names. Until he found his own. At number six in the second. WISEMAN.

He turned, quietly determined, and watched the others saunter off down the corridor.

'My eyes are dim I cannot see,
I have not brought my specs with me.'

David smiled wryly, and took a deep breath.

'I have not brought my specs with me.'

* * *

That evening after the children had gone to bed, Ruth cautiously entered the dining room. So much was going on. She wanted some contact with her husband.

Victor, pencil in hand, was bent over the table totting up numbers in his ledger-book. Piles of invoices were scattered over the dining table.

'What are you doing?' asked Ruth.

Victor didn't answer. He continued his calculations.

'Accounts,' said Ruth, answering her own question. She hovered for a while.

'Not now,' muttered Victor.

Ruth flushed pink. 'I'll do some ironing,' she said.

* * *

David and Judy squatted down behind the coffee table in the Samuels' front room. They both had their homework books out. David was helping Judy with her sums.

'Two hundred and sixty-four,' pronounced Judy.

'That's it,' said David. 'See. You've got it.'

She smiled at him proudly.

'Do you know this one?' asked David.

'Which one?'

'It's rude.'

Judy looked at him curiously. He sang softly.

'Hitler, he's only got one ball.

Goering's got two but very small.

Himmler, has something similar,

But poor old Goebbels,

Got no balls,

At all.'

He grinned at her shyly. But Judy's eyes were tearing up.

She sang,

'One little, two little, three little golliwogs.

Four little, five little, six little golliwogs.

Seven little, eight little, nine little golliwogs . . .'

She turned to David. 'At school, they sing it all the time,' she said. 'Because I don't know their silly skipping songs.'

David tried to think of the right thing to say. 'I bet you know lots of things.'

Judy thought for a second. 'I read, I write, I know my tables; my bible. I can milk a goat; sew a dress; birth a calf; plough a field.' Her eyes lit up, then clouded over again. 'They don't ask me what I know. They don't ask me anything.'

She lost herself in her thoughts.

David knew what she was talking about, what it felt like never to be asked about anything that didn't fit in with what everyone else did. It had never occurred to him before that anyone might possibly think of doing that. But why shouldn't they? After all, wasn't that part of what made people interesting, how they were different from you? Wouldn't it be boring if everyone was the same?

'So, was it Hitler that killed your grandparents?' Judy asked.

'I suppose so,' said David. He contemplated for a moment. 'Yes.'

They returned quietly to their homework.

Dennis in his work clothes put his head through the door. 'I'm off now,' he said. He seemed unusually anxious.

'Judy, you OK? David, you need food?'

'I'm fine thanks, Dennis.'

'Loretta out back if you need her. Grace sleeping upstairs. Is your mother home, David?'

'Making my birthday cake. I think. It's secret.'

'A lovely woman. Free-spirited. You look after her,

won't you?'

'Yes, Dennis.'

'Good boy.'

Dennis looked from David to Judy and back again. A lump came into his throat.

'You going to go far, boy. You going to get opportunities. Cos no-one has to know who you are. If you want. Where you come from. Understand me?'

'Yes, Dennis.'

'Don't squander them, you hear, those opportunities.'

'No, Dennis.'

Dennis swallowed the lump in his throat.

'And don't take no notice of anything I say, will you, David?'

'No, Dennis.'

'Good.'

twenty-two

David closed his eyes, and took a deep breath to steady himself. This was his first opportunity, his big trial. Dennis had talked him through it. Now he was ready. Mr Pugh, who was umpiring at the bowling end, gave him his line. He squared up determinedly to the bowler. Fisher was the first team's number one. He was fast, very fast for a young player.

Fisher and Jessop, the wicket-keeper, exchanged knowing grins. Jessop leant in close to David. 'I thought your job was scoring, Wiseman. Too much for you, was it?'

'Sort of,' replied David.

Fisher didn't bother with his normal long run-up. He sent down an accurate but medium-paced ball. David lifted his bat and cracked back a fierce drive that went whistling low to Fisher's left.

'Stop it!' shouted Jessop.

Fisher tripped over himself as he lunged for the ball. He missed it.

'Drat!'

David smiled inwardly as he and the other

batsman darted up the pitch. They took a couple of runs, and he prepared to face Fisher again.

'Lucky shot, Wiseman,' said an incensed Jessop.

'Knock his block off, Fisher,' yelled one of the other fielders.

'Give him one of your killers.'

This time Fisher was more determined. The ball zipped down. David played it carefully and defensively away. Fisher and Mr Pugh looked at one another with raised eyebrows. This was not the Wiseman that they were expecting.

The game continued in the same vein. David picked his shots carefully, taking few risks. As Dennis had instructed, he kept his concentration focused on the ball and hardly glanced at the score. 'No-one can walk past me' was the watchword. He wouldn't be dislodged. At the end of the innings he was still there, unbeaten. He walked off the pitch, to considerable applause from the rest of the second team. He allowed himself a look to the scoreboard. It read 'LAST MAN not out 42'. He could scarcely believe it.

Mr Pugh stood waiting, hands on hips, at the edge of the pitch.

'Forty-two runs,' he said. 'Useful innings,

Wiseman. It's done you a lot of good, watching the first every week.'

'Yes, sir,' said David. 'No, sir. Thank you, sir.'

'It wasn't a fluke, was it, boy?'

'No, sir.'

Mr Pugh shook his head wonderingly. 'Miracles do happen. The Junior Challenge Cup beckons, even for you, Wiseman. We're short a solid middle-order batsman.' He hesitated for a moment. David held his breath. 'I'll give you a go.'

'Wondrous,' said David as he walked away. 'Wondrous oblivion.' Pugh started in disbelief.

The rest of his team thronged around David, even the disgruntled Fisher patting him on the back.

'What did Pugh say, Wiseman? Are you in the team?'

Reece shook him firmly by the hand.

'Great show, Wiseman. Didn't know you had it in you.'

The boys made their way back to the changing-room, David at the centre of an admiring crowd. 'Where did you learn strokes like that, Wisey?'

'Where are you going to play him, Reece?'

David drank in the adulation.

twenty-three

Well done, David. Now you are ready for the next level.'

Dennis stood over David and Judy in the back garden. They looked back up at him expectantly. He held an open book in his hand, for all the world as though he were about to marry them. He tapped the page with his finger.

'Dennis's bible. C.L.R. James. This man is like Moses to me. He's a political theorist and the best cricket writer in the world. Listen to this.' Dennis read from the book. *'Another name for the perfect flow of motion is style, or, if you will, significant form.'*

Dennis picked up his bat and swung it around easily and flexibly in his wrist, as if it were a drum major's baton. In the next-door garden, Victor stopped his weeding to listen.

'We are talking about an art form, children, a form that flows. Like dance. Like music.' He waved the bat mesmerically, making patterns in the air. Ruth watched in a reverie from David's window. She caressed her bare arm.

Dennis made a show of yawning, and continued the motion. 'See. Just do like this. Nice and loose. Easy. Easy. You got to relax, feel the thing deep inside you.'

David and Judy picked up their bats and started to swing them around in imitation. David furrowed his brow.

'Let go, boy,' said Dennis. 'You know the trouble? You got the strokes, now. But you thinking about them too hard. Your brain ticking too fast. You can forget about the strokes. Free yourself up a little.'

David nodded, watching the bats together weaving patterns in the air, giving himself over to the magic of the movement.

'Yes, David. Yes, Judy. Easy now.'

The three bats were somehow bound together, yet separate. Connected, but different. Together they made star shapes, ellipses, figures of eight. Time slowed down. David felt himself relax, sink into his body. There was nothing in his mind but the motion of the spinning bats. Victor gazed, spellbound, on the other side of the fence.

Dennis's eyes twinkled. 'See, people,' he said. 'You growed up a little. Now it's time to be a child again.'

He picked up the ball.

'Let's play,' he said. 'And I mean *play*.'

They spent the next two hours playing comedy cricket. Charlie Chaplin cricket. Keystone cops cricket. Buster Keaton cricket. Every ball that was bowled they took a swing at. Whether they hit it or not, they ran. Or hopped. Or jumped. Or pirhouetted. Or skipped. Or tumbled between the wickets. They hit fast balls, slow balls, imaginary balls, backward balls, sideways balls, even upside-down balls. They whooped and cheered and laughed and hollered themselves hoarse. They played cowboy cricket – if a ball hit the wicket they pretended to be shot down dead. They played pirate cricket, pretending to hang from the net. They played Jewish cricket, nodding up and down like men in prayer. They played ska cricket, undulating like limbo dancers. They played themselves silly.

* * *

David jigged up and down in front of the record player in the Samuels' front room. The song was a Mickey Katz up-tempo comedy number, a spoof of *The Marriage of Figaro* in gabbled English and Yiddish. It came to a helter-skelter finale. David lifted the needle off the worn 78, and laughed out loud. He turned to a bemused Judy.

'Like it?'

'Sure.'

'It belongs to my parents.'

Judy picked a disc off a pile on the floor. 'Here. Listen to this one.'

David sat down while Judy put the record onto the portable. It was a ska number, Sugar Dandy, with a strong back beat, lilting and jaunty.

You're my, you're my sugar-dandy

You're my, you're as sweet as candy

After a few moments of listening and swaying to the beat, Judy began to dance. She pumped her hands up and down and jiggled her hips, moving to and fro with all her young grace in front of an increasingly excited and captivated David.

You're my, yes you've touched my heart

You're my, right from the start

She stopped and put her hands on her hips. 'Come on!'

'I can't.'

'What you say?' she reprimanded him.

She reached out her hands to him and pulled him out of the chair. David jigged up and down awkwardly. She took hold of his hands and began the pumping action to help him find the beat. He soon got the feel for it. Judy let go and David continued on his own.

Your kisses so sweet, it thrills me so

Eyes are like beautiful diamonds

I'm yours, you're mine till the end of time

You should realise, we were meant to be

She spun and twirled in front of him. He remained inimitably David. But he kept the beat going and found some ease of movement. She turned back to face him. They grinned at one another shyly.

twenty-four

The milkman was down the end of the street, almost finished his round. From the bedroom window Ruth heard the front door shut below her, and watched Victor, David and Lillian leave the house. She waved but they didn't turn round. It was supposed to be her day to come to the shop. She had told Victor that she had a headache and would join him later.

She pulled a cotton dress gently over her head. It was a tight-fitting dress. She liked it. It wasn't flashy, but it showed her shape. She still had a shape, even after the children. She ran her hands slowly over her body, smoothing out the fabric wrinkles. She was in a kind of dream. She had thought about nothing but this moment for days. Now that it was here, there was a kind of unreality about it.

She heard the Samuels' door slam. She watched through the net curtains as Grace and the girls headed up past the corner shop. All clear. The street was quiet.

She slipped quickly out of the front door and across to the Samuels' house. She knocked, gently but urgently. Dennis opened the door. He wore his work trousers and a white singlet.

'Ruth? What is it?' Dennis pointed embarrassed to his singlet. 'Excuse me. I'm not long back from the foundry.' She slipped quickly past him. 'Yes. Come in, come in.'

The sun spilled through the kitchen window. A yearning Elvis Presley ballad echoed on the radio. Dennis began to fumble with the teapot.

'Have a seat, Ruth. You'll have some tea? Now where is the tea?' He rooted around in the cupboard. 'Is this it? Yes. You want some tea?' He began to search for a teaspoon. Ruth approached his broad back and put a hand on it. She put another hand on his arm to stay him. He quieted at her touch.

'Ruth?' he whispered.

Slowly he turned around in her arms. She looked up to him, searching his eyes. He brought his head down to hers and they kissed, long and slow, gently finding one another. Ruth was trembling. They stood pressed against one another and the trembling subsided. She took a half-step back. She touched his chest, wonderingly. His arms around her could feel her tense body through the thin dress.

In a moment they were kissing again hard, hot and fiery. Ruth whimpered.

Dennis pulled back abruptly. He put his hands up, palms forward, as if to ward her away. He struggled to contain his breathing.

'We can't do this, Ruth,' he said. 'We got to stop before we get started.'

She stared at him wide-eyed. 'Don't you want me?' Her big brown eyes filled with tears.

Dennis smiled. 'I do, Ruth.' He looked at her. 'Of course I do. You're beautiful. And nice.' She was beautiful and nice, and he wanted her. A lot. He had never been so tempted. He thought about the shifts he and Grace worked, the strain they'd been under, of finding a home, settling in the girls, she never seemed to have time for him; time to be close; or him for her, come to that. And then there was their religious differences, she a churchgoer, him not; and . . . But that was just it. Grace was his life.

'We're married, Ruth. We're married people.'

He took her in his arms again and held her. Ruth nodded her head through her tears. She did her best to still herself. She stroked his midriff curiously. He stroked her arm. She looked up at him. 'I haven't lived yet, Dennis.'

Their eyes met. Dennis nodded, understanding something about this strange woman.

'I love you, Dennis,' she said. She reached forward to kiss him again. Dennis kissed her back, unable to resist. Then he held her gently away from him.

'Sure you do. Sure you do.'

* * *

Victor sat in his office. It was end of day quiet. The lights were out in the shop and he was ready to leave. In one hand he held a poison pen letter, written on the familiar blue writing paper. It screamed in large letters TIME IS RUNNING OUT, YIDS. In his other hand he weighed David's cricket ball. He tossed it gently in the air and caught it. He tossed it higher. It stung his hand. He tossed it higher still, and dropped it.

'Oops!' he said.

He bent down to pick up the ball. He crumpled up the letter and threw it in the wastebasket.

twenty-five

Tuesday. Team announcement day. Released from his lesson, David made a bee-line for the cricket notice-board. Jessop and Hargreaves were just leaving. David barged through them.

'You don't want to know, Wiseman,' teased Jessop.

'Nice one, Wisey,' said Hargreaves.

David took a deep breath. There was a match this week, against another North London school. His finger tracked slowly down the names. There he was. At number six. Wiseman. Pugh had kept his word. He was in. David flushed with quiet pride.

That evening he didn't go next door, but practised with the team. Ruth tucked him blearily into bed. She kissed him tenderly.

'My hero,' she said.

David lifted his head from the pillow. 'Mum?' he said.

'Yes.'

'Do you still love Dad?'

Ruth coloured up. 'Yes. Of course. Why?'

'I just wondered,' said David. 'He's always at

the shop. He doesn't ever play. Dennis would be better.'

He nuzzled under the blanket. Ruth looked at him, dumbfounded.

She paused for a moment to pull herself together at the top of the stairs. Then she slipped quietly into the front bedroom. Victor was kneeling on the floor on the other side of the bed. He hadn't heard her. He had two teams of matching buttons laid out on the carpet in front of him, much like David with his cricket cards. In his hand was an open book, which he was fully absorbed in.

'The laws of cricket number thirty,' he read. 'Blah blah blah . . . if the ball should pass the striker without touching his bat or person, and runs be obtained, the umpire should call or signal bye.' He waved his hand as if saying goodbye. 'So that's it. Bye!' He waved again. 'The over is over. All change please. Oy. What a game!'

He shuffled the buttons around, getting himself in a right mess. Ruth noticed at Victor's bedside that book by C.L.R. James, *Beyond a Boundary*, Dennis's Bible. The secretive schmuck! Why hadn't he said something about wanting to learn about the game that so enthused his son? Her heart warmed to him.

He could be as soppy as the next man if he wanted to. She opened the door wider and then shut it firmly to indicate her presence.

Victor turned and looked up to her guiltily. 'Just looking for a button,' he said. 'For my coat.' He became aware of her compassionate radiance, turned upon him. His voice went hoarse. 'I thought I had one.' He swept up the buttons. 'I'll get one from the shop.'

* * *

The street was quiet, lit by moonlight. The church clock struck two in the distance. A dark-clothed figure made his way up the road. He was bouncing a rubber ball and catching it again. Deliberately. Rhythmically. It was Mrs Wilson's grandson. He stopped opposite the Wisemans' house. He bounced his rubber ball hard off the front garden wall. It echoed menacingly into the night. He did it again; and again.

Victor, awake and restless anyway, heard the rhythmic thump. He slipped out of bed quietly so as not to disturb the sleeping Ruth, and gently drew aside the curtain. He peered out. The young man had caught his ball, and stared threateningly back up at Victor, right in the eye.

Victor held his gaze. The young man slowly clenched his fingers in the shape of a gun, and lifted his arm to aim it. Straight at Victor. He looked fixedly along the sights. Victor remained unmoving. The young man fired the gun. Pow! Victor didn't flinch.

Ruth stirred in her sleep. She lifted her head off the pillow. 'What is it?'

Victor continued to stare down the young man.

'Nothing. A cat. Go back to sleep.'

Ruth turned back over and snuggled down in the bed. The boy pocketed his imaginary gun, and walked away. Victor let the curtain drop.

twenty-six

The big day had arrived. David's twelfth birthday. Not as big a day as his next birthday, his thirteenth, his barmitzvah, for which he would have to do a lot of work, and for which he would get loads of presents which he didn't want from all kinds of relatives and acquaintances of his parents whom he had never seen. This was to be a big day in another way. It was the first time he had ever invited a bunch of the boys from school to make the long trip south over the river. What was even more impressive was that a lot of them were coming.

That's what was worrying Ruth. Getting it right for them and their parents.

The dining room table was laid for a birthday tea. Ruth, in a smart blouse and suit, was busy arranging serviettes, straightening the cucumber sandwiches, and slicing the chocolate cake. David appeared in the doorway. He looked the model of cosseted decency. Ruth didn't look up.

'Did you change your shirt?' she asked him.

'Yes, Mum.'

'The one I put out?'

'Yes, Mum.'

His hand reached out for a crisp. She slapped it away.

'And your socks?'

'Yes, Mum.'

'Brush your hair. It's sticking up.'

How did she know? She hadn't turned round to look at him yet!

'I've brushed it.'

'You want to look a schlemiel in front of your friends? Brush it again.'

'Do I have to?'

'You have to. Use Daddy's Brylcreem. What's the time?'

David peered at his new watch. 'Ten to three.'

'Victor! Where are you?' yelled Ruth. 'Get down to the station. It's ten to three. You want them to turn around and take the next train back home?'

Victor appeared in the doorway. 'I'm going. I'm going.'

She bustled through to the front room. Through the window she could see Victor getting into the Hillman. Was this the man she wanted to spend the rest of her life with? She fingered the curtains

152

nervously and brushed an imagined smear off the window.

Mrs Wilson and Mrs Dunkley were standing in front of Mrs Wilson's house keeping a watchful eye on the proceedings. A large blue Rover rounded the corner. 'Oooh, la di da, now we've got bloody royalty,' said Mrs Wilson. The car pulled up. Jessop emerged from the passenger side. The driver's window rolled down, revealing his mother, young and elegantly attired. She looked disdainfully up and down the street. Ruth bustled David up the front path.

'Go and hold the door for the lady.'

David ran forward to open the door. Mrs Jessop pulled it shut again, dragging David almost off his feet.

'Thank you, I won't get out,' said Mrs Jessop.

'It's so good of you to bring Toby,' said Ruth. 'Are you sure you won't come in for a cup of tea.'

'Very kind, I'm sure. But I have to run. See you later, Toby. Be a good boy.'

Mrs Wilson and Mrs Dunkley were much amused. 'To-by,' they echoed, smirking at one another. The car roared off.

The other guests soon followed. Several boys

arrived together with Victor in the Hillman. They greeted David with much ribaldry and backslapping and handshaking. One boy was dropped off by a chauffeur. Ruth threw Mrs Wilson a victorious glance. Bloom arrived, accompanied by his father. David hadn't forgotten the incident with the desks. He had particularly wanted to invite Bloom, who had been very quiet at school since then.

The last boy to come was the captain, Reece. He arrived in a modest car, a Ford Popular, driven by his mother. Just when Ruth had given up trying to offer parents hospitality, Mrs Reece got out of the car and brought her son into the house herself. She seemed to Ruth friendly and without airs, almost normal.

Ruth and Mrs Reece stood in the doorway of the front room and watched David joyfully receive his presents. Other boys larked around, or examined those that had already been opened.

Ruth tried once more. 'Would you like a cup of tea,' she asked.

'No thank you, but . . . I wonder if I could use your toilet.'

'Certainly,' said Ruth. 'Let me take your coat.'

Under her coat, Mrs Reece wore a sweater and

jeans. Pinned to the sweater was a black and white badge with a peace symbol on it. Ruth blinked. She couldn't take her eyes off it.

'It's the Campaign for Nuclear Disarmament,' explained Mrs Reece.

'Of course.'

Ruth directed her through the kitchen. As Mrs Reece disappeared into the bathroom, Victor came the other way carrying a tray of glasses. Ruth turned to him anxiously. 'I didn't think to polish in there.'

'The woman has other things on her mind.'

In the front room, the boys were admiring David's presents. The globe of the world, the new set of stumps, the motorised glider.

Jessop nudged the boy next to him. 'Did you see, David's got nig-nogs living next door?' He grabbed at one of David's presents.

'Look at this, Fish. It's a magic set.'

He opened the lid. Bloom reached in and took a pack of playing cards.

'Choose a card,' he said.

'You are a card, Bloom,' said Fisher.

'Ha ha.'

Hargreaves took a card. 'The queen of hearts.'

'She stole some tarts,' said Fisher.

'You've got tarts on the brain,' quipped Jessop.

Mrs Reece emerged from the bathroom. 'What a very nice house you have,' she told Ruth.

Ruth was stunned. 'Thank you so much,' she said. It was all she could do to stop herself from curtseying.

'I've got a few tickets for the Lord's test next week,' said Mrs Reece. 'I know David loves his cricket. Would he like to come?'

'Yes. Yes. YES!' shouted David, who had just been opening Reece's card with the ticket inside. 'Wow! Look at this, Mum. Thanks, Reece. It's my best present ever.'

Ruth smiled with satisfaction. She crossed to the window to wave goodbye to Mrs Reece. 'Thank you very much, James,' she said. 'It'll be a wonderful day.'

David crossed to the mantelpiece to put the card and the ticket on display. The gabble continued around him.

'This is a funny globe,' Hargreaves was saying. 'I can't find England.'

'It's on the other side, you nana.'

'All I can see is Siberia where Wiseman comes from.'

David gasped. Through the window he glimpsed Judy coming along the street. She wore a gay print dress, and carried a parcel, all ribbons and bows. David looked around him desperately. Ruth was busy picking wrapping paper off the carpet. His father was out the back somewhere.

The doorbell rang.

'I'll go,' said David.

Ruth looked up from the floor. 'I don't suppose any of you like cake,' she teased the boys.

'Not half,' they chorused.

David opened the front door. Judy waited expectantly.

David looked at the floor, then back at Judy. 'I can't really play right now,' he stuttered. 'I've got my friends here. Later.'

Judy stared at him, unbelieving. She thrust his present into his hands. 'Happy Birthday,' she said, eyes smarting, and turned quickly on her heels. David hurriedly closed the door.

Judy ran back along the street.

The boys were gathered around the dining table, singing Happy Birthday. David sat the head. The cake, decorated painstakingly by Ruth with icing stumps and bails, bat and ball, was lit with its twelve candles. Reece as captain took on the mantle of conductor. Jessop had organised the boys into a variation on the old words.

Wondrous oblivion dear Wiseman
Wondrous oblivion to you.

David blew out the candles and the boys cheered. His mother kissed him and his father patted him on the back. He seemed happy but a little absent from the ribaldry, a strange stillness about him. The shouts echoed around him.

* * *

The next afternoon, David, in his cricket gear, left his own front door in the usual way, and approached the Samuels' door, ready for the regular practice. He knocked, and waited, for what seemed like a long time.

Grace opened the door. David was about to say hello, but Grace cut across him.

'She doesn't want to play with you today,' she said. 'She don't want to play with you any day. So you can take your bat and go play somewhere else.'

Grace closed the door. David blushed scarlet. He remained poised for a moment, then turned on his tail, ran, and let himself in his own front door. He scurried up to his room, and dived onto the bed. He buried his head in the pillow. The strains of Lillian's mournful cello penetrated from the next room.

twenty-seven

The next day the school cricket nets were a hive of activity as the teams practised for the culmination of the season. David had told his mother that morning at breakfast that he would be late home every day that week because of cricket practice. This wasn't true – there wasn't practice every night. It was a way of covering up the fact that he would no longer be going next door. He threw himself into the afternoon's practice, desperately keen and involved, chasing after every ball and chucking it back to the bowler as though his life depended on it. Reece blocked a ball and David made a mighty dive for it, almost succeeding in catching him out.

'It's only a practice, Wiseman, you nana,' yelled Jessop.

David grimaced and rubbed his bruises. He stayed until the last ball was bowled.

By the time David got on the train it was late, rush hour. At the station he joined the stream of commuters filing past the ticket barrier. He hung back, in no hurry to be home. Ahead of him a group

161

of young men, among them Mrs Wilson's grandson, were approaching the black ticket collector. They brushed past him rudely. Mrs Wilson's grandson, who was the last, barged heavily into him.

'Tickets, please,' said the ticket collector. 'Let me see your tickets, please.'

'Sod off, you wog,' said one boy.

'Tickets, please,' said another boy, mimicking a Caribbean accent.

David watched, clutching his season ticket, from behind the barrier. Some other commuters, impatient, slipped on through, dropping their tickets on the floor. Mrs Wilson's grandson watched coolly.

'Show me your ticket, please,' said the ticket collector, grabbing one of the youths by the arm.

'Get your filthy hands off me,' said the boy. He pulled away sharply and drew a switchblade from his pocket. It snapped open. The last of the commuters hurried past the barrier. The youth waved the thin blade in front of the black man's face.

'Don't touch me, coon,' he said.

'Go back to your own country, wog,' said another youth.

'He hasn't got one.' They laughed. The ticket collector looked on helplessly as the boys backed away, holding out the knife threateningly. They turned and ran whooping out of the station.

'Bastards,' said the ticket collector, stooping down to pick up the scattered tickets from the floor.

David approached the barrier. 'You can check mine if you like,' he said. He held up his ticket for inspection. The inspector's eyes were hurt and angry.

'Get outta here,' he said.

David walked rapidly, stiffly, towards home. When he approached the Samuels' house he sped up almost to a run. His head looked down at his feet. Invisible. He slipped quickly into his own front door.

He peeked surreptitiously out of his bedroom window. Dennis and Judy were out practising in the net.

'Not bad,' Dennis was saying. 'Not bad, not bad. Come right forward on those balls and kill the spin. Kill the spin.'

He took hold of the bat from behind her and demonstrated what he meant.

It looked to David as though nothing had ever happened; they had never met; he had never been there. He slunk back quickly into the shadows.

He missed seeing a concerned Grace sitting on a

tea-chest near the bowler's run-up and watching over the practice.

'You think she's all right now?' she murmured to Dennis as he prepared to bowl the next ball.

'Yeah, man. She gonna be all right. Give it time, eh?' He didn't sound too sure.

After dinner, David looked out again. The practice net was empty. The posts creaked and the net billowed in the breeze. His cards lay scattered on the floor. He kicked them uninterestedly. He picked up Judy's present and finally unwrapped it. It was a record, the ska record that they had danced to together. He took it downstairs. Victor and Ruth were talking intensely in the kitchen. Thank goodness they were so absorbed in themselves at the moment. He slipped into the front room.

The needle dropped onto the record. The ska beat began to thump out of the radiogram. David turned the sound down low.

You're my, you're my sugar dandy
You're my, you're as sweet as candy

He sat listening, his head in his hands.

* * *

It was the day of the match against the other North London school, the game David had been selected for. His team was batting and had just lost two cheap wickets. Now it was David's turn. He marched robotically off the pavilion steps, his bat tucked under his arm.

'Go carefully, David,' Reece told him. 'Steady the ship. This bowler isn't so hot.'

'Good luck, Wiseman,' said Hargreaves, the batsman he was replacing.

The words passed him by.

He took the crease, and banged the bat down hard to make his mark. He wiped his brow. The weather was hot and sultry, as if before a storm. He'd hardly found his middle when the ball came down fast. David blinked his eyes, took a dab at it, and missed. He muttered to himself.

The next ball came down. This time David was ready. He took an angry swipe at it. It clattered to the boundary. A cheer came up from the watching boys. David flexed his shoulder-muscles. The next ball, a similar one, went smashing to the other boundary. The boys applauded, but Reece frowned. He shook his head worriedly at Mr Pugh.

David was oblivious. All he wanted to do was to smash that ball. The third one came down faster. But David picked his spot. He seemed to have all the time in the world. It was sweet and it was powerful. It soared over the head of the long off fielder and bounced into the bushes. A six. The boys cheered wildly.

The final ball of the over was a slower one, cleverly flighted. David, anger spent, poked at it without resolution. It clipped the bails.

'Howzat!'

David walked unmoved back towards the pavilion. The watching boys shook their heads in dismay. 'Hard cheese, Wiseman,' they said. 'Good try.' David took his seat. He didn't care.

'Bit erratic for you, Wiseman,' said Mr Pugh. 'Not quite the innings we needed. Still, fourteen runs. Not bad.' He fixed David with his eye. 'It's a big game next Saturday. Stay cool for that one, eh.'

'Yes, sir.'

'Win that and we've won the cup. Are you with me?'

'Yes, sir.'

There was scarcely a breeze in the air.

* * *

David sat on his own in the library, his homework books in front of him. All the other boys had left. He'd taken to coming here after school on days when there wasn't a match practice. He could hear the cleaners with their mops and buckets in the corridor. The sun slanted low through the window. The teacher in charge started to pull down the blinds. The keys jingled in his hands.

'Got a home to go to, Wiseman?' he said. 'Because if you haven't, I have.'

David packed away his things and left. He approached a motley group of four or five boys behind the bins in a remote corner of the playground. They were the malingerers, with quiffs in their hair, skewed ties, and incomplete uniforms. Fox was there, his big bulk squatting on a low wall.

'What are you doing here, Wiseman?' he said. 'Not cricket practice. You weren't on detention, were you?'

Baxter took an ostentatious drag on his cigarette. 'Wiseman's too good to get detention.'

'Do you want a ciggy, Wiseman?' asked Fox.

'No thanks.'

Baxter waved his cigarette in David's face.

'Smoke it, go on.'

David shook his head. Baxter brought the cigarette closer, right in front of David's eye.

Another boy called out. 'Master coming.'

A teacher was emerging from the door across the playground.

'Let's go,' said Fox.

The boys loped off round the corner. David stood alone in the large empty playground. The sky rumbled.

* * *

The rain lashed down on the empty net next door. The sodden mesh sagged in the middle. David watched from his window. The water spattered off the pitch. It bounced off the tea-chests. There was a loud crack of thunder. The rain came down still harder.

* * *

Ruth peered through the raindrops on the car window as the wipers swished from side to side. Victor drove the Hillman, cruising slowly through leafy suburban streets. The large and sedate houses slid by.

'That's a nice place,' murmured Victor. 'With a sign up.'

'It's too big. You're so . . . why should anyone need such a big place?'

Her gaze followed the well-proportioned, solid house as it disappeared behind them. It had a wisteria draped gracefully over the front porch; and a little first-floor balcony, with ivy hanging down.

The rain began to lighten.

twenty-eight

The Queen was being presented to the West Indian players. Frank Worrell, in his blazer and whites, was leading her down the line. She shook hands with each of them in turn, to polite applause. She stopped to have a conversation with Garry Sobers.

It was tea-break at the Lord's test, England versus the West Indies. David was there with James Reece and his mother. The ground hummed with excitement, but David looked subdued.

'She looks quite like you, Mum,' offered James.

'God forbid,' replied Mrs Reece. 'Would you like an egg sandwich, David?'

'Have one of mine,' said David. 'I've got hundreds.'

It was true. He pulled out a huge bag of sandwiches supplied by the anxious Ruth. David munched his way through them mechanically, his scorecard on his knee.

The game resumed. A huge clamour of whistling, stamping and drumming erupted from the West Indian crowd below. The Caribbean supporters –

many of them recent immigrants – had stunned the sedate English cricket-lovers with their loud enthusiasm and repartee. Their team had taken the game of cricket by storm with its daring, athletic and stylish play. With it came the joyousness of their followers, anxious to prove a point to a mother country which hadn't proved as maternally welcoming as they had imagined.

Gibbs sent down a quick one. Cowdrey drove it stylishly for four.

'Good shot,' said James.

'Wizard,' said David.

At the front of the noisy crowd, sitting on a rug on the grass, were Dennis, Judy and Mr Johnson. Dennis took a long swig of his beer. A pile of empty bottles sat by him.

'All the politeness over with now,' Dennis exulted. 'Watch Wesley and Lance rough them English batsmen up a bit.'

'Hall going to break Cowdrey now,' said Mr Johnson. 'I lay a bet on it.'

'Cowdrey's very clever,' said Judy.

'Clever is one thing. Fast is another,' said Dennis. 'Which side you on, sweetie?'

Cowdrey played the next ball comfortably away.

Then Hall sent down a fast ball which bounced up high and struck the batsman on his forearm. Cowdrey dropped his bat and clutched his wrist. He sank kneeling to the ground, in obvious pain.

'Oh no, not Cowdrey,' despaired Reece. 'We need Cowdrey.'

'Still another two hundred to make,' said David.

Cowdrey was helped off the pitch.

'Don't tell me that's fair, Dad,' said Judy.

Dennis was chastened. 'He didn't mean to hurt him. Just intimidate him a little.' He put an arm around his daughter. 'Cricket can't be pretty pretty all the while,' he said gently. 'Sometimes it's rough out there.'

David went to the refreshment kiosk to join the queue for ice creams. He turned away from the booth with a large cone in each hand – ninety-nines, with chocolate flakes – to see Dennis, laden with bottles of beer, coming towards him from the bar area. David froze in his tracks. Dennis greeted friends on the way.

'You all right, man?'

'Good, man, good.'

Dennis spotted David and came to a halt in front of him.

'Well, well, well.'

David stared up at Dennis, speechless.

'What you looking at, boy?' said Dennis.

David stayed lost for words. His eyes wandered to the beer in Dennis's hands.

Dennis lifted the bottles. 'Mind your business, David,' he said. 'I got plenty reasons to need a drink. Because a man got to survive in this shit-hole country some damn way. Right? *Right?*'

He glowered at David. David turned on his heels and ran.

'Damn,' muttered Dennis. He hadn't meant to frighten the boy. But David did need to be called to account. 'You can enjoy your ice cream, David,' he hollered to David's retreating back. 'But we have some very serious talking to do.'

David disappeared into the crowd.

*   *   *

Reece and his mother brought David home in the Popular. Ruth met them at the front gate. David, exhausted, fell into his mother's arms.

'Thank you so much,' said Ruth.

'Our pleasure,' replied Mrs Reece.

'David?' said Ruth.

'It's a close game,' said David. 'But the West Indies

are winning.' Ruth nudged her son. 'Oh. Thank you for having me.'

Dennis and Judy turned the corner into the street. They had left early to avoid the crush, and taken the tube.

Ruth was peering at Mrs Reece's CND badge. 'I wanted to ask about your brooch,' she said.

'Badge.'

'The bomb. It's a terrible thing. Do you have meetings?'

'And lectures. Would you like to meet for a coffee one day? My name's Barbara, by the way.'

'I'd be delighted, Barbara.'

Victor came to the front door. He held his arms out to David. 'Come on then, young man. Bed for you.'

David pushed past him and made his way upstairs. James and his mother climbed back into the Popular. Barbara wound down the window.

'I'll call you.'

'Thank you.'

The car puttered away. Ruth followed it with her eyes. She became aware of Dennis and Judy approaching. She watched them for a moment, strangely moved. Dennis glanced up in Ruth's direction. Embarrassed, she stepped hastily inside.

Dennis put a protective arm around his daughter as he led her up the front path.

'Home,' he said.

twenty-nine

The distant bells were calling congregants to church. Ruth was hanging out the washing, slowly and deliberately, glancing from time to time over the fence. She glimpsed Dennis at the kitchen window, and busied herself sorting clothes. He opened the back door and stood filling the doorway, a small glass in his hand.

Ruth put down her pegs and approached the fence. 'Cup of tea?' she said tentatively.

'What, Ruth?' He drew nearer.

'Cup of tea? I'm on my own.'

'The girls out too,' said Dennis. 'But no, no tea, Ruth.'

He held up his glass, rum. 'You want one of these?'

'No, thank you.' Ruth put her hands on the fence and searched for the right words. 'I wanted to say sorry,' she said.

'I'm glad to hear it. I guess it was one of those things. Nothing meant.'

'That's the trouble, Dennis. I did mean it. If I didn't it would be easier.'

Dennis frowned. He took a sip of rum. He was beginning to realise that he and Ruth were talking about different things.

'You ... stirred up so much in me,' Ruth explained. 'Don't get me wrong. I'm glad.'

Dennis smiled wryly. Ruth continued.

'When I came here I was David's age. My parents ... they couldn't get out of Germany.' Dennis nodded sympathetically. He wondered where this was leading. Ruth continued. 'I worked for an English family. Couldn't wait to leave there. Nobody taught me how to ... be a woman. I always make a fool of myself.'

Dennis shook his head. 'You're not a fool, Ruth,' he said.

Ruth glanced towards the house. 'He ... he's trying now, trying his best. With David. Me.'

Dennis nodded slowly. 'I thought we was going to talk about another matter,' he said.

'I'm so sorry, Dennis,' Ruth said.

She tore herself away and ran towards the house. Dennis watched her go. He clenched his fist and cracked the glass he was holding. The clear liquid dribbled down.

* * *

A group of boys sat round the table in the rabbi's gloomy dining room. Yasha hovered over David, who had announced to his astonished parents that he needed to attend the discussion group now, since this was his barmitzvah year. It had seemed another good way of getting out of the house and avoiding the issue of Judy and Dennis. But now it came to it he was bored stiff and Judy and Dennis were all he could think about.

'So what do the commentaries, the gemara, tell us about the forbidden days for sexual union?' asked the rabbi, a small man with an uneven growth of beard.

The boys tried to suppress giggles.

'Saturday afternoon, sir?' suggested one boy. 'My dad's mad on football.'

Hilarity exploded all round, except for David, who had missed the joke. He didn't even smile.

thirty

Dinner was over. Lillian was clearing the table, Ruth washing up. Outside it was beginning to get dark. David was in the kitchen listening to the Archie Andrews show on the new transistor radio. Ruth couldn't see the point of a ventriloquist doing a radio show. David couldn't make her understand that this was exactly what made it funny.

David's father came off the telephone in the hall. He came beaming into the room, his chest puffed out. He motioned to David to turn down the radio.

'Ladies and gentlemen!' he said.

Ruth and Lillian stopped what they were doing. Victor looked towards David.

'Ladies and gentleman! Listen, please. I wish to make an announcement.'

Lillian and her mother exchanged apprehensive glances. Victor continued.

'We can exchange contracts on the Hendon house this week. We can move in three weeks' time.'

Lillian clapped her hands. 'Hooray!' She grinned at her mother. Ruth smiled back despite herself.

'I never thought it would happen,' she said.

Victor eased himself into a chair.

'Your mother chose a nice new house. In North London,' he explained to David. 'Near your cousin Simon.'

Lillian jumped up and down excitedly. 'When can we see it?'

'In good time,' said Victor. 'In good time.'

'How much did it cost?'

'I hate to think,' interjected Ruth.

David stood up, slowly. The words echoed around him.

'I'm employing a manager for the shop,' explained Victor. 'And opening a new branch in North London. You can take the tube to school.'

'I saved some tea-chests at the shop,' said Ruth. 'You can have one each for your toys.'

'I don't have toys any more, Mummy,' said Lillian.

David muttered under his breath, 'I'm not going.'

'David,' asked Ruth. 'What did you say?'

'I'm not going.'

He ran out of the door, and thundered up the hall.

'I'M NOT GOING.'

He pelted up the stairs.

'I'M NOT GOING. I'M NOT GOING.'

He ran into his room, and slammed the door hard behind him.

Victor, Ruth and Lillian stared after him.

'David?' said Victor. He glanced at his wife and pulled himself out of the chair.

'DAVID!'

David stood in his room, breathless, close to tears. From next door came Dorothy's faint cries and the click of ball on bat.

Victor's heavy tread advanced up the stairs. He opened the door without knocking.

'GET OUT!' exploded David.

'David!'

'I'm not going. I'm not interested in snobby North London, with those snobby rich children. No-one asked me. I'm staying here!'

'Listen to me!' Victor said.

'Those people think they run the world. They think they run everyone. They bully people. They tease people. They try to make you feel small. Well I'm not going. Do you hear? I'M NOT GOING!'

The words poured out of David. His eyes were brimming with tears. Victor stood, shocked. Ruth called him from the top of the stairs. 'Victor!'

Victor stepped back out of the room. David listened to Ruth's muffled whispering on the landing.

Victor reappeared in the doorway, Ruth at his shoulder. His tone was conciliatory.

'David. It's for you we are doing this. Understand.'

David snorted. 'So you should grow up with other Jewish children,' Victor continued. 'Here is no life for a Jewish boy.'

David glared at him in silent rebellion. Victor abandoned his efforts to be reasonable.

'David! You'll do what you are told!'

David came rushing towards him in a rage. Victor and Ruth stepped back involuntarily. David slammed the door, and locked and bolted it.

Victor rattled at the handle. 'David! Open that door!'

David ran to the bookcase and seized his Surrey bat. He beat the bat on the bed in frustration, yelling, 'The only people who ever bothered about me are here! The only friends I ever had are here! And I sent them away! You let me send them away!'

Ruth gasped. The light was beginning to dawn.

'Don't talk to me like that, young man!' Victor shouted. 'I work my socks off for this family. Ow! OW!!'

Victor suddenly checked his movement, his head cricked to one side.

'What is it?' asked Ruth.

David paused for breath.

'My back,' said Victor. 'My back's gone.'

'David, please . . .' called Ruth.

Lillian shouted up the stairs. 'He's always spoiling things. It's not fair.'

'I'm not going,' said David, sinking onto the bed.

'Help me,' groaned Victor. Ruth put his arm over her shoulder and helped him shuffle to the top of the stairs.

'Ow. Ow,' he groaned.

It was nearly dark in the bedroom. There was a gentle knocking at the door. Ruth called tenderly.

'David . . . David . . .'

David's pillow was sodden with tears. He blinked his eyes.

'David . . . Do you want a drink?'

David shook his head.

'David?'

'No.'

'Will you let me in?'

'No.'

Victor called softly. 'David?'

'Oh, you're there too.'

'I should have spoken to you about it before. Given you some warning. I didn't want to worry you. I thought it would be a nice surprise.'

'You don't know me,' replied David.

Victor's knuckles gripped the banister rails.

'I'm not going,' said David blankly.

'You can still see your friends,' said Ruth. 'Judy. Mr Samuels. At the weekend. We'll talk to them. Explain.'

'No. Don't,' said David firmly. 'Anyway, Dennis. Dennis his name is. You should know.'

'What does he mean?' Victor asked Ruth. 'What's he talking about?'

'Night night now, David,' Ruth butted in hastily. 'We've got lots more talking to do in the morning. Sleep well. Big day tomorrow.'

'Goodnight, David,' said Victor. 'Sleep well.'

David listened to his father's tread, limping awkwardly downstairs, his mother following.

'Well tell me, Ruth.'

'Ssshhh. Nothing to tell.'

David lay back down on the bed. The wind rattled the windows. It was a restless night.

The boys got off the train with Mr Pugh. He looked smaller than usual, smaller than they were. He had a satchel on his back. They ran past him on the stairs, laughing and jeering at him. He looked sorry for himself. They had to leave him behind. He couldn't keep up.

Then they were going through the ticket barrier. David worried that they didn't have enough tickets, but the burly black ticket inspector didn't try to check them, he stood there expressionless like stone and they breezed on past, running like the wind.

They ran out of the station exit and into a kind of cloud, a bright white light. Suddenly David found himself on his own, the other boys had fallen away and he was jogging out onto a cricket pitch. His bat was under his arm. It felt glorious, he was suffused with joy; a glorious moment of utter happiness. The whole West Indian cricket team was there, in their blazers and caps, all the names he knew, Worrell and Hall and Gibbs applauding him and welcoming him to the crease. He took his stance. Judy was at the other end in a bright yellow dress, and she was skipping, but she didn't have a skipping rope. She had a bright smile fixed to her face. And that's where it started to feel wrong. Garry Sobers had the ball in his hand. He grinned – that was nice – and bowled down a ball. And then it all went sour. David took a mighty swipe at it, and it sailed into the air, but when he looked up it was a knife, not a bat he had in his hand. The hilt glinted in the sunlight and the blade was thick with blood.

thirty-one

David shifted restlessly in his bed.

A dark-clothed figure crept around in the darkness of the Samuels' garden. He poured liquid from a petrol can, one line running towards and under the back door, and one line running towards the posts that held the net. He splashed liquid under the windowsills, and over as much of the net as he could reach.

He stopped and listened to the silence.

He struck a match, and held it to the liquid. Lines of flame rushed quickly towards the kitchen door and back towards the garden. It lit him up momentarily as he scampered over the garden wall and out of sight.

Flames licked greedily up the cricket net and around the back door. They crept along the windowsill, and into the kitchen itself. The wind fanned them into a blaze.

The light from the flames gleamed on David's window. David's eyes blinked into wakefulness. They focused on the flickering glass.

He leapt out of bed and rushed from one window to the other, drawing aside the curtains. The net was burning fiercely. The kitchen was ablaze.

David threw open the sash and leaned out.

'Dennis!' he shouted. 'Judy!'

The house was still. Just the crackling of the flames as they began to spread. Suddenly there was a muffled explosion in the kitchen, and a wall of hot flame shattered the glass in the windows. The gas had caught.

David shouted again. 'DENNIS!'

There was no response. David raced for his treasured box of cards, and tipped it upside-down on the bed. The cards scattered every which way, and out came his precious cricket ball. He snatched up the ball, rushed to the window, spat on it and rubbed it on his trousers. He took careful aim and chucked it at the window opposite. It looked for a horrible moment as though it might fall short. But it didn't. The window smashed noisily.

'JUDY!' David yelled.

Judy's bleary face appeared through the smashed glass. The flames flickered on her nightdress. She wonderingly took in what was happening.

'Quick!' shouted David. 'Wake up your mum and dad! Get everyone out!'

He stepped back, embarrassed, away from the window. He watched Judy disappear rapidly behind the curtain. David took a deep breath. He unbolted his door.

Victor had called the fire service. Once everybody was safely out of the house, he and Dennis had got out the garden hose and played it on the kitchen and the hissing net until the firemen arrived with their more substantial tackle. Victor and Dennis were half-dressed, caked with sweat, bedraggled and filthy.

The firemen got the gas turned off. They ran their hoses down the alley by the side of David's house and then across David's back garden. It didn't take them too long to bring the flames under control, but there was still a lot of steam, smoke and fumes coming from the building. They said it wasn't safe yet.

The fire engines blocked the street at the front, a police car in front of them with its flashing blue light. Firemen were coiling up hoses. A large crowd of neighbours, including the Wilsons and the Dunkleys, stood observing with hushed excitement and curiosity. Grace and the three girls sat watching, huddled in blankets. Ruth and Lillian brought them cups of hot tea and biscuits. David, shy of the Samuels, had slipped back into his house and watched from the upstairs window. Victor beckoned him down. It was still dangerous. David slipped down to join his sister among the crowd.

Dennis, soot-covered and stripped to the waist, was talking with one of the policemen. Smoke still tumbled from the open front door.

'When will the investigation be starting, officer?'

'What investigation would that be, sir?'

'The fire in my house.'

'Sir, I think you'll find that's an accident.'

Dennis started to get angry. 'An accident? That's one house I see on fire, you know. It's the one house in this street on fire.'

'Can I ask you a couple of questions, sir. Does anyone smoke in the house?'

'Nobody smokes.'

'Nobody smokes in the house?'

'Nobody smokes.'

'Did you have a chip pan on or anything?'

'For what?'

'Well for cooking chips, sir. For cooking.'

'We were sleeping, man. The family was sleeping.'

Dennis was getting more and more exasperated.

'Sir, have you got an open fire?'

'No, man.' Dennis strode over to Grace and the girls. He was spluttering with rage. 'You hear him? You hear him? I got my family here. I nearly lose them in that fire.' He strode back to the policeman. 'You see them, my wife and children?'

'Sir, would you calm down?'

'No! I won't calm down. I won't calm down.'

'Restrain yourself.'

'Restrain myself?'

'Sir, I'm asking you . . .' The officer put his hand on Dennis's arm.

Dennis freed himself angrily. 'The people that caused this. It's them should restrain themselves.'

Victor placed himself between Dennis and the policeman. 'He's right, officer.'

'You telling me it's an accident?' roared Dennis. 'This was no accident.' 'He turned and marched angrily up the garden path towards the front door. 'I can prove it to you.'

A fireman called out, 'Don't go in, sir. The fumes.'

Dennis disappeared into the thick black smoke.

Grace let out a despairing wail and rushed after him. Ruth and a policeman held her back.

The house went quiet. The crowd waited in stunned silence. One fireman conferred hastily with another, who went to fetch some breathing apparatus. The seconds ticked by.

'Ruddy idiot,' muttered the policeman. The remaining firemen shifted uneasily on their feet. Ruth held firmly onto the sobbing Grace. Smoke continued to swirl from the open door.

Victor could bear the waiting no longer. He pulled a handkerchief out of his pocket and ran up the path. He ducked into the smoke. Ruth and David started forward, gripped with anxiety. They heard his cries.

'Dennis! Dennis!'

Inside it was near dark and impossible to breathe for smoke and fumes. Victor peered in the front room. Nothing. He stumbled up the stairs, rushing from room to room, holding the handkerchief to his mouth, coughing and calling out. He heard a faint thump from downstairs and clattered back down. He ducked his head and staggered towards the kitchen where the smoke was thickest. He kicked open the door and crawled in. Dennis was lying wheezing slumped on the floor beside the dresser.

Victor tried to pull him up, but his back wouldn't hold, and he was beginning to feel faint. To his great relief a fireman in a breathing mask came crashing up the hall.

'Here,' Victor gasped.

Victor emerged, rasping from the smoke, then Dennis, holding onto his shoulder, and then the fireman, under Dennis's other shoulder, and holding a spare mask over his face. David and Ruth watched, wide-eyed and relieved. Grace ran forward.

'Dennis!'

Dennis looked up, let fall his mask, took a great shuddering breath, and smiled at her. Victor's eye was caught by Dennis's hand, draped around his shoulder. Dennis was clutching a bunch of charred but familiar-looking letters. Victor caught Dennis's eye. He nodded in recognition.

Dennis stood up and threw the letters one by one towards the crowd and the watching policemen. 'You see this? And this? And this? This is what me, my family are living with.'

Ruth was shocked, amazed. She felt proud of her husband's bravery. But how come she hadn't known that any of this was going on? One of the letters fluttered to David's feet. The words were clearly visible. GO HOME NIGGERS.

'This is what we living with,' repeated Dennis, and sat back exhausted with Grace on the garden wall. Loretta, Judy and Dorothy ran to join them. They huddled around their father.

Victor turned to the crowd. 'You should be ashamed,' he said. A tear fell from Ruth's cheek. 'We should all be ashamed.'

His father's words pierced David like a knife. His face was white. When he thought about the party . . . it might as well have been he who started the fire.

Mr and Mrs Wilson start to sidle away. Victor pointed at them accusingly. 'Ask those two, officer,' he proclaimed. 'Ask them about their grandson.' The crowd turned to look.

Mrs Dunkley stepped forward out of the crowd. She picked up Loretta's cup of tea and proffered it to Dennis. Dennis took hold of it gratefully.

'Got anything stronger, Victor?' he whispered.

thirty-two

Ruth straightened David's tie.

'Are you sure you don't want me to come?'

David shook his head.

'Dad's at the police station. He said to tell you good luck. Have you got your prayer book?'

'Yes.'

'Good luck twice, then,' said Ruth, taking him by the arms and kissing his forehead, twice. 'One from me, and one from Dad.'

'Thanks.'

The chapel was decorated gaily with streamers, Union Jacks, and murals of biblical scenes. It was jam-packed for the annual prize giving. Children were standing at the sides, David, the minister, and the other VIPs were in the front row, the rest of the congregation behind them. Mrs Jackson was addressing the gathering from the dais.

'Now the prize for scripture learning for the young ones.' She looked around the room. 'We are very honoured to have here to present the prize a good friend, also a hero of the hour, David Wiseman.'

There was loud applause as David made his way up to the dais.

Mrs Jackson continued, 'David is a Jewish boy, as was our Lord Jesus.'

David gravely shook Mrs Jackson's hand and picked up the prize. His eyes scanned the audience, searching the faces.

Mrs Jackson read from a piece of paper. 'The prize go to Wilhemina Jones.'

A cute and chubby little girl, in pigtails, made her way through the clapping crowd towards the dais.

'Where are Dennis and Grace?' whispered David to Mrs Jackson.

'Still with the police, I think.'

David's face fell.

'Judy and Dorothy here though. Look.'

David's eyes found Judy and Dorothy. For a moment he caught Judy's eye. She turned away. David's face burned. Wilhemina waddled on-stage and David handed her the brightly wrapped prize, to more applause.

Mrs Jackson surveyed the crowd jubilantly.

'David will now recite for us Psalm 23,' she said.

'The Lord is my Shepherd, in the original Hebrew, which I am sure will be an education for us.'

David placed his prayer book on the lectern, took a deep breath, and started to chant melodically.

'Adonai ro'i, lo ech-sar

Binot deshe yah-bitzeini al mei mnuchot y'na-ha-leini.'

A humming came from the back of the hall, and merged harmoniously with David's singing. It was the congregational choir, dressed in flowing purple robes. They started to sing in English, their own melody counter-pointing with David's.

The Lord is my Shepherd

I shall not want

He maketh me down to lie

In pastures green

He leadeth me

The quiet waters by

The effect was beautiful. David's voice, strong and clear. The choir, with its deep bass and rich harmonics, ebbing and flowing around him. The congregation were filled with wonder. David's eyes brimmed with bitter tears.

* * *

Victor sat at the kitchen table. Ruth stood behind him, gently massaging his shoulders.

'Ow!' he said. 'Not there. Further over.'

She tried another place.

'Lower,' he said.

'Here?' asked Ruth.

Victor beamed. 'That's it. Yes. Lovely. Not too hard.'

Lillian's cello swooped and soared.

'More, please,' said Victor. 'Oh my God, that's good. Ow!'

Ruth removed her hand. 'No,' said Victor hastily. 'Don't stop. Please. Don't stop.'

Ruth laughed, and then went quiet, thinking about her son.

thirty-three

David plucked up his courage. It was time he got this over with, once and for all. He was frightened, but the experience of the chapel had given him strength. He knocked, tentatively, at the Samuels' front door. The doorframe and sills were black with soot. The small front garden was trampled and strewn with the debris of the night. Grace cautiously opened the door. Her apron was filthy and her sleeves rolled up to the elbow. She saw David and relaxed.

'Hello, David.'

'Hello, Mrs Samuels. Are you . . . all right?'

'We alive,' said Grace. 'We still got a house here. More or less.'

She smiled at him. 'That was a good throw, David. We thank you for that.'

David's serious face looked up at her. She couldn't help warming to the boy. 'Dennis and Judy out back. Come through.'

David entered and Grace threw a wary glance up to the window opposite. A curtain stirred. She firmly closed the door. They were going to keep their wits about them now.

Loretta and Dorothy were sweeping the stairs. Grace guided David down the damp and grimy corridor, past their silent, watching eyes, past the watching eyes of Mr Johnson and other friends who had come to help them repair the damage. The kitchen was charred and blackened almost beyond recognition. He could see Dennis and Judy through the smashed glass, forlornly dismantling what was left of the net.

He stepped out into the garden. The tattered and blackened remnants of the netting hung limply in the air. Judy raked the scorched grass. Dennis threw a piece of charred post onto the pile and looked over. His boiler suit was filthy black.

'Hello, David?' he said.

'Hello, Dennis, Judy.'

Judy carried on with her raking, head down. David took a deep breath, and launched in.

'I'm not a hero, Dennis.'

Dennis nodded thoughtfully.

'My parents are moving house and they didn't tell me . . .'

Judy slowed up her raking. Grace emerged from

the back door, followed by Loretta and Dorothy. They stood and listened.

'I want to stay here. Where you are. You are the only proper friends I ever had. I never meant to . . . I'm sorry about the party. Really I am. It was stupid. It wasn't because she's . . . She's too good for them – not the other way round. I want to live next door to you, go on playing cricket . . .'

David ran out of words.

Dennis threw another piece of netting on the pile. David grew suddenly anxious. Dennis approached David solemnly.

'I hear what you telling me, David. And you know what?'

David shook his head. Dennis held out his hand.

'I admire a fellow who can admit his mistakes.' He shook David's hand gravely. 'Judy took it very hard, David. My whole family did.' He looked towards Grace and the other girls. They nodded assent.

Judy stopped her raking.

'I'm so sorry, Judy,' David said.

Judy stood unmoving. Dennis walked over and put an arm around her.

'Judy,' he said. 'Do you accept David's apology?

This is your choice, you know, and if you don't want to, you don't have to.'

He stepped away from her. 'It's up to you.'

Judy thought for a moment. What David did had hurt a lot. It had felt like a real betrayal of their friendship. But she could see he hadn't meant to cause her pain. And now he was sorry. She could forgive him.

She walked over and offered him her hand. He shook it earnestly. Judy stepped back.

'David, you have to go with your parents,' said Dennis. David flinched.

'Your parents are very, very good people,' continued Dennis. 'I am sure they have their reasons. And I know they got your interests in mind. It may not look like that from where you stand.' He looked to Grace. 'It may not be any better. It may be worse. But it's what you got to do next . . . and then you learn from that.'

David looked close to tears again.

'We're going to miss you,' said Dennis gently. 'We'll miss you a lot.'

He put one arm around David's shoulder, one around Judy's. Dorothy ran to join them. David looked from one to the other of them.

'What about you?' he asked. 'Will you stay?'

Dennis's eyes strayed to the tattered nets. It seemed for a moment like some of the fight had gone out of the big man. Then he looked back to his daughters.

'We're right here to stay, man,' he said firmly. 'We're here to stay.'

Grace and Loretta nodded assent.

'Tell you what,' continued Dennis, smiling broadly. 'We got a bit of a picnic thing coming up. It's a very, very special do. I want you to come, and why don't you bring your whole family?' He grinned at David. 'On Saturday.'

David's jaw dropped.

'Saturday . . .' he said falteringly.

thirty-four

Ruth and Victor were rummaging around among the junk, rolls of old cloth, and boxes of knick-knacks in the basement stockroom. Victor pulled at a roll in the dim light.

'I told you we still had it,' he said triumphantly. 'See, throw nothing away.'

Ruth fingered it sceptically. 'I should throw you away, you cheap good for nothing Polak,' she said. 'It's rotten.'

Victor's shoulders slumped. Ruth sniffed at her fingers disdainfully.

'We'll order new,' said Victor, brightening up. 'Woodberry is here.' He called up the narrow stairs. 'Mr Woodberry, sir!'

The familiar smoker's croak emerged from the shop. 'Yes, Mr Wiseman.'

'I have a commission for you.'

* * *

Saturday, the day of the big game was fast arriving, and school cricket practice was becoming increasingly intense. David stood by the nets and

207

watched the play swirling around him. He had become a valued member of the team, taken seriously by his fellows. The biggest game of their season was approaching. How could he let them down? And yet . . . how could he let Judy and Dennis down again? He knew one thing. He was going to have to make a decision. And he was going to have to make it soon. This was agony.

Meanwhile Victor had left the shop early. He and Ruth were knocking on one door after the other in the street, and talking to the neighbours. They separated, to cover more houses. But for Ruth there was still a sweet feeling, of executing a plan together. A joint plan, for once. She glanced towards her husband, knocking on a door up the street. He wasn't a bad man. He did his best. She felt a rush of warmth towards him. And then it went. She was angry too. There were still things to sort out between them.

A perplexed Reece was listening to David.

'Something more important has come up,' David was saying. 'And . . . that's it, Reece. That's all. I can't play.'

'But it's the Junior Challenge Cup,' said Reece. 'What can be more important?'

'You'll have to take my word for it. I'll explain to you one day.'

David anxiously watched Reece's face for signs of rejection. Was he going become a nonentity again, a laughing-stock among his classmates?

Reece's face relaxed.

'It's OK. Vikram can have a game,' he said brightly. 'Have you got that "Ska" thingy record with you, by the way? I'd dig borrowing it.'

'Have you got your Elvis?' asked David.

thirty-five

Loretta opened the Samuels' front door and motioned the neighbours quickly inside. Mr and Mrs Dunkley were among them, and the Cartwrights from across the street, but not the Wilsons. They were nowhere to be seen that day. Victor stood beside Loretta, ushering people through, and then followed them inside.

* * *

Ruth and David strode across the common. It was a glorious sunny mid-summer's day. David carried a gaily-wrapped present under his arm.

'When's Dad coming?' he asked.

'He's got a job to do,' said Ruth. 'He won't be long.'

They rounded the hill. Spread out below them was the field where the picnic was happening. A steel band was playing, Lillian among them plucking her cello like a bass. Huge amounts of food were being laid out on trestle tables, decorated with brightly coloured cloths. Children ran everywhere. A bunch of cricketers, black and white, in assorted kit, were limbering up and preparing the pitch under Dennis's guidance.

'Wow. Look at that,' said David. 'Wondrous! There's cricket. Why didn't you tell me? I haven't got my kit.'

Ruth opened her big bag. Folded inside were David's whites. 'Da-daa,' she said.

They joined the throng. Ruth swayed and shimmied Caribbean-style to the beat. She waved to Grace behind a food table.

'Grace! It looks wonderful. I'll come back in a minute and have some.'

'Make sure you do!' said Grace. 'You want a pattie, Mr Johnson?'

Mr Johnson offered his plate for the third time. David greeted Judy and they went to get kitted up. Dennis approached Grace as she dished out patties.

'You excelled yourself here, Mrs Samuels.'

'Thank you, Mr Samuels,' said Grace, with a flirtatious smile.

'Give me another one of those delicious patties,' asked Dennis.

'Mind you don't get fat on me now,' teased Grace.

'I begin to wonder if you stop noticing,' said Dennis.

Grace smiled at him shyly. 'Not likely, Mr Samuels!' she said.

Judy and David sat under a tree together. The dappled sunlight played on their faces. They seemed a little older as they padded up, ready to open the batting. David shyly held out the present to Judy.

'This is . . . this is for you.'

Judy carefully unwrapped it.

'I can't take this. This is your Surrey bat.'

'That's all right,' said David. 'Have it, really.'

Judy put the bat back in David's hand, and held it there.

'It's OK, David,' she said. 'We're friends now. Keep it, David. Please.'

David held onto his bat, with a tinge of relief. They stood up and surveyed the scene.

'I've never played with grown-ups before,' said David anxiously.

'They aren't grown-ups,' said Judy. 'They're friends of my Daddy.'

David held out his hand.

'Good luck!' he said.

Judy leant over and kissed him on the cheek.

'Good luck!' she said.

* * *

Judy was facing the batting again. It was a widish ball, which she turned expertly down the leg side.

'Shot, sweetie!' shouted Dennis from behind the wicket, abandoning his loyalty to his side for his pride at his daughter's prowess. 'Run, man, run.'

She and David took the run and it was David's turn to face the batting. He glanced up to the brow of the hill. His eyes lit up. His father and a whole bunch more neighbours were walking down to join the party. He waved to his father, and his father waved back. Dennis ran to welcome them.

'Come here, Victor, come here,' he called. 'Do me a favour, stand right there by the fence and fill that hole she keep finding.'

Victor trotted to the edge of the outfield to guard the boundary.

'Good, man,' said Dennis. 'Now stop the ball.'

Ruth wandered over to stand by Victor. She had taken off her coat to reveal a large CND badge pinned to her sweater.

'It's done,' Victor said.

'Good,' replied Ruth.

'And I booked the removal men.' He watched David and Judy excitedly running between the wickets. 'But did we make a mistake? Should we stay?'

'No,' said Ruth. 'It's too late now.'

'I wouldn't like the Wilsons to think they'd got rid of us.'

'I don't think they will.'

'I just wanted a nice place. A nice area. I was poor a long time.'

Ruth took a deep breath. 'Why didn't you tell me, Victor? About the letters. Why?'

'I didn't want to worry you.'

'I'm not a child any more, Victor. I'm not the girl you married.'

Victor realised the truth of what she was saying. He reached out and took her hand in his.

'You're not. It's true. You're a lot more than that now.' He paused, and they watched David block another ball. 'Ruth . . . the house . . . Without you . . . it means nothing.'

Ruth nodded quietly. 'I know.'

A stylish two-tone convertible cruised through the entrance gate on the other side of the pitch and pulled in next to the steel band's white van. Two men in blue blazers began to get out. All heads turned towards the car. An excited murmur riffled through the crowd.

'It's Garry Sobers.'

'And Frank Worrell.'

'What are they doing here?'

Dennis ran over to greet them.

'Hey, Frank. What time you call this?' he called, pointing to his watch. David's eyes jumped out of their sockets.

'How's it going, Dennis?' said Frank, as he was mobbed by a posse of youngsters wanting autographs.

'Those two pipsqueaks hogging all the batting, man,' said Dennis. 'Garry, do me a favour and bowl down a few for these children, you hear.'

Garry ambled towards the bowling crease.

'Run, man!' called Dennis. 'We're in trouble here.' Frank settled down in the crowd with a beer. The bowler tossed Garry the ball. All eyes turned towards the game. David stood transfixed. This was his dream. Exactly. He couldn't believe it.

'Get yourself ready, David,' came Dennis's voice from behind him. 'It's you and Garry Sobers now.'

Abruptly David realised that this was not a fantasy and that the best all-rounder the game had ever seen was really about to bowl to him. He hastily squared up. Garry smiled warmly, and sent down a deceptively lazy ball. David played it late, and managed to miss it completely. It shaved his off-stump. The crowd let out a sigh. David looked around anxiously.

'Don't worry,' said Dennis. 'Don't worry about it. No-one can walk past you.'

He readied himself for the next ball, and found Judy's eye as he did so. She smiled at him, encouragingly. The ball came down a little slower. David played it stylishly towards long off.

'Run, Judy, run,' shouted Dennis. The crowd clapped and cheered. Judy winked at him as they crossed in the middle of the pitch. Victor jumped up and down with excitement.

'That's my son,' he shouted jubilantly. 'That's my son.'

Garry stepped back to take a longer run-up. He wiped the ball carefully on his trousers. The crowd hushed.

'It's your time now, David,' murmured Dennis.

David mopped his brow. He tried to quiet his breathing. What was that other thing Dennis had said? *Don't squander your opportunities.* Well, then . . . he wouldn't.

The outside world went silent. Time slowed down.

He focused all his attention on that little hard lump of dyed leather, in Garry's hand . . .

To an outside observer, the next ball was faster. But for David there was all the time in the world. His back swing was easy and loose, his timing perfect, his drive sweetly struck. The ball rocketed towards his father.

'Victor!' yelled Dennis. 'Stop the ball!'

Victor dithered and danced on the spot, made an almighty dive for the ball, and watched it disappear under his body and trundle on to the boundary fence. The crowd roared with laughter. David whooped and thrust his hands into the air. Victor scrambled to his feet and ran to retrieve the ball.

'Too good,' proclaimed Garry. 'Too good for me.' He gestured towards Frank sitting among his flock of admiring children. 'I been bowling to that ole feller too long. He done ruined me.'

He lifted his hands high in the air, to warm applause.

'Good luck, Garry.'

'Give that England a bashing.'

Victor retrieved the ball from beyond the boundary and carried it proudly back onto the pitch, to much amusement. The umpire signalled the end of the over and the fielding side began to cross over. David ran to meet his father in the middle of the pitch. He leapt into Victor's outstretched arms. Ruth watched moist-eyed with Lillian as Victor swung his son around in a huge bear hug. They clung to one another tight, as the other cricketers moved on around them.

thirty-six

Dennis had his eyes shut tight. Loretta held his arm and guided him out of the back door.

'Mind the step,' she said. 'Mind the step.' She led him out into the garden. Grace and Judy, Dorothy and Mr Johnson followed close behind, giggling in anticipation. 'Can I trust you?' joked Dennis. 'Can I trust you?' Loretta stopped moving and Dennis fell silent.

'You can open your eyes,' said Loretta, and stepped away.

Dennis slowly, wonderingly, opened his eyes.

In front of him was a cricket net, spanking new, glowing in the evening light. It was perfect. Not a hole, not a tear, not a bent nail or a crooked post. The stumps and bails were ready in place. They were new too. Dennis stared, unbelieving. Slowly his eyes brimmed with tears.

He looked around him.

Mr and Mrs Dunkley and some other neighbours were watching from their garden. Dennis nodded in acknowledgement to them.

Another group of delighted neighbours watched from the bottom of the Wisemans' garden. By the washing line stood Lillian with Ruth and Victor, the relieved architects of the plot. Dennis's heart swelled. He gestured his thanks.

David leant out of his bedroom window and smiled.

The net was radiant. Even Dennis's family and those others who had been in on the secret were imbued with its magic. Dennis swallowed hard.

'Grace,' he growled. 'Would you mind please fixing me a very big, strong . . . cup of tea.'

Everybody laughed. Grace took him by the arm. A cork popped.

* * *

The ska beat thumped out from next door. Laughter and excitement, and the thud of dancing feet. David was taking a break from the party. He had something he needed to do. His room was bare, apart from his bed and wardrobe and a couple of tea-chests that held his clothes and toys. He looked out of the window at the dancing figures in the Samuels' kitchen, the shadows flitting across the concrete. Victor's loud laughter resounded even up here. He watched as Judy and Dorothy stepped out into the garden to admire the new net. The voices floated faintly on the evening air.

'That Victor, him dance like an elephant,' complained Dorothy.

'Yeah. It's a good party though,' said Judy.

'Look at the new net, now,' said Dorothy.

'I can't wait to try it out tomorrow,' said Judy. She looked up and caught David's eye. They smiled at one another.

David sighed. He plucked up his courage one last time.

Four hundred and thirty-six cricketers were spread out in front of him. They covered practically the whole floor. He laid down the last one. It was that battered old card, W.G. Grace, the master, with his big black beard. He folded his huge arms and tapped his foot. All eyes turned to David.

David plunged in. 'This is how it is,' he said. 'I'm going away soon. And you're not coming with me. So this is . . .' he hesitated '. . . goodbye.'

The cricketers murmured their shock and dismay.

'The end of the innings,' said Grace.

'I'm sorry,' said David.

'I might have seen it coming.'

'Don't worry,' said David. 'I'm going to leave you in safe hands.'

The players sighed with relief.

'You're too old for us,' said Grace, the light dawning.

'Yes.'

David looked away.

'What is it, lad?' asked Grace.

'The team,' said David. 'They lost the Junior Challenge Cup.'

'And you weren't there. Hmm.'

'I let them down.'

'No, you didn't,' said Grace. 'You played the game. You showed us all the way it should be played: straight bat, head up . . . that's more important than a silver bauble.' He turned to the players gathered around him. 'Come on, boys,' he murmured, and began to clap, loudly and steadily.

'Goodbye, David,' he said.

Sobers next to him took up the applause. 'Good luck, David.'

David beamed.

Peter May put up a hand in farewell and began to clap. So did Walcott and Worrell. Hutton joined in, Compton and Bailey, and the Bedser twins. Then

Ramadhin, and Statham, Cowdrey and Roper. In a few moments the whole cavalcade were applauding David enthusiastically.

David soaked up the acclamation.

'Goodbye, young David.'

'Well played, sir.'

'Well bowled.'

'Give it to them, David.'

The applause became an ovation. The ovation became a roar.

David's eyes streamed with tears.

thirty-seven

That night, before they tucked them into bed, Ruth and Victor began telling Lillian and David about where they had come from. Their heritage. Because it was very late, they intended not to say very much. But they ended up talking into the early hours. They gathered around David's bed. Victor told David and Lillian about his parents, their grandparents, and the religious life of the Polish village he had grown up in. Ruth told them about her irreligious parents – and their comfortable but increasingly dangerous life in a German city. The children listened quietly. For once Lillian was too sleepy to pretend to know it all.

Ruth described her journey to England at David's age, leaving her parents behind at the train station. She described the strange English family she lived with during the war, who expected her to work for her keep, but who were kind sometimes as well. Victor said he had been in the Polish Army and then escaped the Germans to join the British Army. He said he had forgotten a lot about the war, and that he would tell them about it another time. In fact, Victor could never forget, but nor did he like to remember; some of his memories were so terrible that he needed time to work out what he could share with David and Lillian.

The hardest part for Ruth and Victor was explaining about the round-ups and the ghettoes and the camps where David and Lillian's grandparents had been murdered. Ruth managed to speak without crying, but Victor cried so much he had to go out of the room. He apologised and said he hadn't cried since nineteen forty-five, when he had first heard what happened. Since then, he had been too angry to cry. But he was crying now because telling the children had made him realise that the chain wasn't entirely broken; his relief and happiness at that had unleashed his sadness and loss. Which he was glad about. He felt better for being able to cry. In spite of everything life went on.

Ruth and Victor wanted to say something about Judy's heritage too. How black people from the Caribbean had joined the British army to help fight the Nazis. And how a few years back, when Britain was short of labour, they had advertised in the West Indies for people to come and work in transport, and nursing, and engineering. That's when Dennis and

Grace had come. Like the Wisemans, the Samuels had been separated – but hopefully they would all be together again one day, including Judy's grandma.

David said he knew most of that already.

Indeed, as he fell asleep David realised that he was no longer in a state of oblivion. Well, not completely. There were always going to be things he would be unaware of, otherwise there would be nothing left to learn. And that, probably, was one of the wondrous things about growing older: there would always be more to discover. But he was glad he knew a few things now, more than he knew before. Maybe if his parents continued to tell him things, life wouldn't be quite the fog of confusion it had been before.

There was one thing he would be able to tell other people, for the rest of his life. Most of them wouldn't believe him. Certainly they wouldn't when he went back to school – he had scored a boundary off Garry Sobers!

* * *

The sparrows chirruped. Grace emerged from the front door carrying two huge bags of clinking bottles, left from the party. A removal van sat outside the Wiseman house, almost loaded, the men drinking tea. This was it: moving day. David had a lump in his throat when he woke up, and it wouldn't go away.

Dorothy was squatting on the grass in the back garden and thumbing raptly through her cricket cards. She began to lay out a team. David gave Judy his new address and phone number. The old gang was gathered in the net.

Victor took the bat for the first time. Judy sent a ball down. Victor wafted at it and missed. The ball rolled gently into the back of the net.

'I'm a hopeless case,' he said.

'No, no, no, Victor,' said Dennis, retrieving the ball. 'This is a good school. The best.'

'Your turn, David,' said Victor, offering his son the bat.

'No, Dad,' said David. 'Let me show you.'

He stretched his arms around his father, much as Dennis once did, and demonstrated the stroke.

'Bat straight. Head up. Watch the ball. And remember: no-one can walk past you.'

Victor repeated dubiously, 'No-one can walk past you.'

Dennis gave the ball back to Judy. 'Underarm,' he murmured. 'Take it easy.'

He looked over to the Wiseman kitchen window, where Ruth was unhooking curtains. She saw him and stopped. She looked beautiful, more a woman now, he thought. Ruth looked carefully about her to make sure there was no-one looking. She blew him a kiss and a tiny wave goodbye. Dennis smiled and nodded shyly.

The next ball Judy bowled Victor clouted into the roof of the net. He galloped gleefully down the wicket. David and Ruth clapped and cheered. Judy eyed the shot with mock disbelief.

Dennis pumped Victor's hand. 'I think we made a bit of progress here,' he said.

David looked to Judy. He suddenly wanted to cry with happiness.

Victor joyfully threw the ball high into the air. It slowed. Then it seemed to hover for an instant at the peak of its ascent. David loved that moment, the red leather ball suspended in the air, before it began its journey down. He wished it could last for ever.

BEND IT LIKE BECKHAM

Narinder Dhami

Jess's parents want her to be a nice, conventional Indian girl. They pray she will settle down, study for law school and learn to cook the perfect chapatti.

But Jess has other plans. She wants to play football like her hero, David Beckham. After all, anyone can cook aloo gobi, but who can bend it like Beckham?

So when she gets talent-spotted by Jules, she grabs the chance to join the local women's team. Now she just has to keep it a secret from her family. And the fact that she's being coached by a gorgeous Irish guy called Joe. Who obviously she's not remotely interested in . . .